# DETECTIVE MCKNIGHT
# DEADLY ENGAGEMENT

## BY DEEZIGN MYSTERIES BOOK 1

### DEE MCQUEEN

# Copyright

Detective McKnight- Deadly Engagement By Deezign Mysteries Book 1
Copyright © 2023 by Dee McQueen
Cover Design By Miblart.com

For more information, email bydeezign@gmail.com

# DEDICATION

*In loving memory of my father James McQueen for teaching me to always finish what I started no matter how difficult it may become and for forcing me to watch Columbo with you even when I didn't want to which was the beginning of my love for mysteries.*

# CHAPTER 1

Morgan was once again awakened by those piercing blue eyes that occasionally would pop up in her dreams to remind her of who she really was. She was sweating, and her heart was racing as she looked around the room. The last thing she remembered was the man she loved with his hands around her neck, trying to kill her. In a panic, she tried to get up, only to be stopped by the throbbing pain in her neck. Morgan was a dedicated runner, so she was used to pain, but this was different. She could usually just grin and bear it, but she felt like she had been hit by a truck.

Morgan lay there in the hospital bed wondering how her life ended up this way. Her engagement party turned into the worst night of her life. Her chest began to tighten, and the tears were streaming down her face like a waterfall; she began to feel an overwhelming sensation of dread, and she sat up holding her chest. Beads of sweat began to cover her forehead. She felt as if a ton of bricks was laying on top of her.

She was very familiar with the feeling of having a panic attack; she experienced them often growing up.

Morgan moved her arms, only to be stopped by the cords that were attached to the devices alongside her bed. She looked towards the door and yelled out for assistance, then she grabbed the remote that was tucked into the side of the bed and repeatedly pushed it.

The annoyed nurse ignored Morgan for a moment and then said, "Hi, can I help you?"

Morgan took a deep breath and said, "Can you please come in here and unhook me? I want to get dressed and go home!"

The nurse replied, "I will be in there momentarily."

Morgan sighed deeply, still irritated and exhausted from the events of the previous night. She felt her wrist to make sure her pink breast cancer awareness band was there, and she began to snap it.

Walking quickly into the room, the nurse said, "I understand that you are ready to leave, but the doctor has not discharged you yet. He wants to observe you for another twenty-four hours."

That was the last thing Morgan wanted to hear. She had work to do. She was a successful attorney with tons of files on her desk, waiting on her to review. Morgan insisted she speak with a doctor. The nurse told her that the doctor was doing his rounds, and that he would be with her as soon as possible.

Morgan looked at the nurse with her big brown eyes and said, "Can you at least unhook me so I can use the bathroom?"

The nurse began to unhook Morgan from the devices. Morgan shifted her five-foot-eleven, toned body to the side, so that she would not expose herself to the nurse as she got up.

Morgan looked over at the door, and a police officer was standing there. She turned to the nurse and asked, "Why is there a police officer outside my door?"

Her nurse responded, "The police stationed an officer here; they wanted to err on the side of caution. We don't want your fiancé to come back and finish what he started."

Morgan grabbed her chest and began to breathe heavily. She began sweating again and looked flushed; the nurse became concerned and asked her if she was ok. She stood behind Morgan and told her to sit back down, because she looked like she was going to faint.

Morgan said, "I am fine. I just realized that my life is still in danger. I can't believe that I have to be protected from the man I was about to marry." Morgan began to wipe the tears as they rolled down her cheeks.

The nurse pushed the dark brown curls that had fallen from Morgan's updo out of her face and said, "I promise you, if your fiancé tries to step foot in here, he'll have to worry about me first."

There was a knock, and the nurse peered through the cracked door. There stood a tall slender man who appeared to be in his mid-30s, wearing a blue suit with a brown and blue plaid Kangol shirt on. He had a badge in his hand. The nurse opened the door the rest of the way, and the man told the nurse that he was a detective, there to interview Morgan Waters.

The nurse walked the detective over to Morgan and said, "Ms. Waters, this detective is here to interview you. I am going to leave now."

The nurse looked at the detective, wagged her finger and said, "Don't be in here too long, and don't upset her. We finally have her vitals stable, and we want to keep them that way."

Wiping his brow with a handkerchief, the detective said, "Hello, Ms. Waters, my name is Detective McKnight, and I have a few questions to ask you about last night—if you are up to it."

She replied, "Yes, that's fine. I just want this over with."

"First, let me say that I am so sorry for everything you are going through right now. It is my goal to find the suspect and arrest him, so that you don't ever have to worry about him again," he replied, as he looked into Morgan's concerned eyes.

Morgan could feel tears about to run out of her eyes, so she turned away from the detective and wiped them away. She then looked at him and said, "Thank you!"

Detective McKnight cleared his throat and said, "Ms. Waters, we have statements from witnesses at your engagement party, and they said that it was your fiancé, Mr. Andre Williams, that they saw fleeing the scene. Can you confirm that for me?"

Just hearing those words made Morgan sick. She picked up the pan beside her bed and began to throw up. Detective McKnight's cheeks filled with air, and he began to gag. He turned his head and put his hands up to his ears. Even though he had three sons, he still could not stand the sound of someone throwing up. Morgan sat back up and wiped her mouth with a paper towel from the side of her bed.

Detective McKnight said, "Ms. Waters, are you ok—do you need me to get the nurse?"

Morgan shook her head and said, "I'm fine."

Repeating himself, the detective said, "Was the man seen fleeing from the scene Andre Williams?"

Morgan wanted to think about anything else but the question that the detective had asked her. She replied, "Yes, it was Andre. He killed that poor man and then turned on me and tried to kill me too. When he was strangling me, all I could see was hate in his eyes. I knew that I was going to die. His eyes...they were so cold. It was as if I was staring into the eyes of a stranger."

Choking up, Morgan said, "I'm sorry, Detective, I thought I would be able to, but I just can't talk about this right now."

"I understand," the detective replied, "this helps me a lot. One more thing, would you happen to have a recent picture of him?"

Looking around the room, Morgan said, "Yes, can you grab my purse off of the ledge?"

Detective McKnight grabbed the sequined black cocktail purse that was sitting on the window ledge. Morgan put her hand into the bag, pulled out her cell phone, and turned it towards the detective; there was a picture of her and Andre the night of their engagement party, both with big smiles on their faces.

Detective McKnight began to contemplate the fact that the hands that were caressing Ms. Waters' waist in the picture would be wrapped around her neck a few hours later. He then asked her if she could send him the picture, so that he could put out a BOLO on Andre when he went back to the police station. He wanted to make sure that all patrolmen were on the lookout for Andre.

Morgan said, "How long will that police officer be here?" referring back to the one outside her room door.

Detective McKnight replied, "The police officer is assigned to you for the next few days for your protection while we are looking for Andre."

Morgan was thankful. She knew that Andre was a dangerous man, and she knew that if he caught up to her, he would not make the same mistake twice—he would make sure the next time, that he killed her.

The two agreed to meet at the police station to complete her interview and file a police report when Morgan was discharged from the hospital.

# CHAPTER 2

Sean didn't know which was worse: the war in the streets, or the one he was fighting in his own home. Sean and his wife, Shelia, hadn't spoken to each other in weeks. Which, for both of them, was a welcomed reprieve from all the arguing they had been doing over the past few months. There had been no peace in their home. Even their three boys, who normally played with each other fairly well, were fighting all the time.

Shelia knew when she married Sean straight out of the police academy that his goal was to be a detective, and that would require long hours and a demanding schedule. In fact, he was an extraordinary officer. His first year on the job, he was awarded a divisional commendation for bravery.

He was on patrol and saw a car on fire on the highway. His quick thinking saved a mom and her newborn baby. Sean quickly moved up through the ranks. Within five years, at the age of 28, he became a detective, and now he is a Detective III, which brought on extra responsibilities.

Sean was no superhero. There were only 24 hours in the day, and his job took up at least 14 of those hours...and that was on a good day. He didn't know what Shelia expected of him and didn't have time to try to figure it out. He had received a call from Ms. Waters that she was going to be released, and that she wanted to finish their interview today.

Sean stretched as he sat up in the bed. He got out, pulled the blanket up and fluffed his pillow. He began to walk over to the closet. As he passed the mirror, he slowed down and admired his abs. There was a time that he could eat a whole pizza and wash it down with a pint of ice cream without having to worry about his weight. Now at the age of 38, if he dreamed about pizza or ice cream, he put on 5 pounds.

Lately, he had been going to the gym more. It had started to become his escape from home. He walked into his closet and began to look around. He rubbed the stubble on his face and remembered that he needed to shave. The closet was usually crammed with clothes, but Sheila moved to the guest room, so now the only clothes hanging in the closet belonged to him.

As he looked around, he began to think that maybe he should have been more understanding. It was a lot on Shelia taking care of their 5-, 8-, and 10-year-old boys. He walked deeper into the closet and began to push aside each hanger while looking through the sea of suits, shirts, and ties. He pulled out his grey suit, that he had tailored to fit just right— when he wore that suit on an interview, he felt like it made him look more authoritative. After shaving and getting dressed, he looked in the mirror and gave himself a nod of approval.

Sean finally made it downstairs. He could smell the bacon and eggs that Sheila had prepared for the boys.

"Daddy! Daddy! Daddy!" the boys yelled, as they ran over and hugged his leg. Sean steadied himself, so that he didn't fall over.

That was the best part of his day. He didn't know what he would do if his mornings didn't begin like that. He loved being a detective, but his greatest accomplishment by far was being a dad, and he took his responsibility seriously, despite what Shelia said.

"Good morning, Sean."

He replied, "Good morning, Shelia."

Sean began to look her up and down. Shelia was still in her pink robe. It flattered her beautiful hourglass shape. She was glowing, and her beautiful dark hair was caressing her high cheekbones. Sean had always been mesmerized by her big brown eyes.

Gazing at her, Sean said, "You look beautiful this morning."

Shelia replied, "Thank you. Would you like some coffee?"

He smiled and said, "Yes, I would love some."

For a moment, it was like old times.

The youngest boy ran and jumped up on Sean's lap. He had cream cheese on his fingers, because unlike his brothers, who loved bacon and eggs, the only thing he would eat for breakfast was a bagel with cream cheese. Sean quickly grabbed his son's wrist and wiped off his hands. The boy masterfully wiggled away from his dad and ran off to play with his brothers.

Sean walked over to the sink and wet a napkin to clean the cream cheese fingerprints off of his suit.

Shelia walked over and said, "How late do you think you are going to work today? I have some errands to run, and I would rather do them without the boys."

Sean said, "I'm not sure. I'm working on a new case and..."

Shelia interrupted him, "You know what? Never mind...why do I even bother."

Irritated with her tone, Sean raised his voice and replied, "Why do you always do that? You turn a peaceful morning into a full blown-out war."

She rolled her eyes and mumbled, "If you thought more of your family than you do your job, we would have no need for this conversation."

Sean stared at her in disbelief and said, "You know what, Shelia? I'll grab my coffee while I'm out."

He looked at his boys. Their bright smiles turned into long faces. The boys hated when their parents argued.

Sean said, "Boys come give me a hug." Instantly, they smiled and ran over to him.

They hugged him and said, "Be safe, Daddy. We love you."

Sean replied, "I love you too. I will see you tonight when I get home."

He turned around to leave. As Sean approached the door, Shelia ran up behind him. Grabbing his arm, she exclaimed, "We need to talk, Sean...I don't know if I can keep living this way!"

He looked at her and closed the door, without saying a word.

# CHAPTER 3

Detective McKnight had walked down the halls of this police station so many times over the years, but something about today felt different to him. He couldn't put his finger on it. He was not the type of person to dwell on negative energy, so he decided that no matter what, he was going to make today a good day.

As Detective McKnight approached his office, he began to notice the familiar smell of burnt popcorn. Every day since the academy, Tony, a fellow officer, had eaten burnt popcorn for breakfast. The whole station smelled like it for the entire morning. Detective McKnight headed towards the break room to get his coffee. He stuck his hand in the blue "sugar container," which was really a broken police union mug, that they started to throw sugar packets in. The cup was empty.

He yelled out, "Aye, Tony! Where's the sugar? This is your month to keep the supplies stocked."

Tony replied, "Sorry, Boss, headed down to the storage room to fill up now."

Detective McKnight replied, "No worries, I'll go. I can use the fresh air. I need to get away from your *stanky* popcorn." They both laughed, as Detective McKnight left the room.

While heading towards the supply room, Detective McKnight saw a tall, confident, well-dressed woman being escorted towards him.

"Hey, McKnight," shouted Sergeant Paddington. "You are just the man that I am looking for. This young lady says she has an 9:00 a.m. meeting with you."

Sergeant Paddington was an old-timer; he had been on the force for decades. The job was his life. He was never married and never had kids of his own. He would joke and say who needs kids when he has a station full of them.

Detective McKnight responded, "Ms. Waters, it's nice to see you out of the hospital, and I hope you are recovering well."

Then he looked at Paddington and asked him to take Ms. Waters to the interview room, because he needed to go grab some sugar.

Paddington looked at him and replied, "Tony is neglecting his responsibilities again, I see, how surprising." They both laughed.

Detective McKnight looked at Ms. Waters and said, "Can I get you anything? Water, coffee, tea...?"

She replied, "No, thank you." As she held up her Ohio State coffee cup.

He smirked and said, "I won't hold that against you. I'm a Michigan fan...Go Blue!"

A few moments later, Detective McKnight opened the door to the conference room and said, "I am so sorry to make you wait. I don't know about you, but I cannot function without my morning coffee."

Morgan said, "I know what you mean. I'm going on my third one of the day."

The conference room was dark and cold. The detectives from the station had requested for the past few years that they paint over the cement walls, so it wouldn't be so uninviting. There was also an old, musty smell in the room. It was the only space available, except for the interrogation room, and Detective McKnight didn't want to take her there...not yet anyway.

"Ms. Waters, how is your morning going?" he said.

Morgan sighed and said, "To be honest, not so good. I am extremely nervous, and I didn't sleep last night. The whole idea of having to relive the most horrible night of my life has me stressed out."

"That is completely understandable. What you witnessed, and what happened to you, was very traumatic, and I apologize that we have to make you bring up such horrific memories. It's best that we interview victims as soon as possible, while the event is still fresh in their minds. How about we just start at the beginning and work our way up to what happened on the night in question." He replied.

Morgan looked up—as she snapped the pink cancer awareness bracelet on her wrist, that she wore in honor of her mother—and said, "That's fine. I'm ready to start."

Detective McKnight reminded her that even though she was not under arrest, she had the right to have an attorney present. She told the detective that she did not need an attorney, but if and when she felt the need for one, she worked with the best attorneys in the state and would consult them, if necessary.

Detective McKnight said, "Before we start, I want to let you know that I will be taping our conversation."

Morgan nodded, and he reached over and turned on the tape recorder.

"Can you please state your name for the record?"

"My name is Morgan Skye Waters."

"Ms. Waters, what is your relationship to the suspect?"

"He was my fiancé."

"How long had you known him before you were engaged?"

"One year."

"Do you know, or have you ever seen the man that Andre is suspected of murdering?"

"No, I do not know the man Andre murdered, though I did see him earlier in the evening at our engagement party, talking to Andre. They were talking like they knew each other. I saw him again when we were finishing our first course at dinner. He sent a message to me through a waiter, asking me to meet him out back, by the guest house. The message said that I should know who I was about to marry. The next time I saw him, Andre was standing over him with a bloody knife in his hand."

"Do you know where Andre is from?"

"He never talked much about his past or his family."

"That didn't seem strange to you?"

"No, Detective, it didn't. I don't like talking about mine either, so it made me feel at ease."

"Ms. Waters, how did you and Andre meet?"

# CHAPTER 4

It all started one year ago...

I popped up and looked at the clock. I couldn't believe I had overslept. The night before, I worked 16 hours getting a brief ready for my boss, Mr. Henry Calloway. That's the price you pay when you are working to become partner. We had a meeting with the client before court, and I could not be late. I jumped into my car, and noticed that I was driving on fumes, so I had to stop at the gas station on my way to the coffee shop so that I could get through the long day that I had ahead of me.

My plan was to get to the firm early, just in case Mr. Calloway needed any last-minute changes on the brief. He is old school, so even though I sent the brief to him via email, he would print it out to read it and mark up the changes that he wanted with a red pen, as if I was still in college. Even though I am like a daughter to him, I work very hard to stay on Mr. Calloway's good side. He is a gruff man, but he is fair. I'll do whatever is necessary to make partner.

As I got out of the car, the smell of coffee beans made me smile. The coffee shop is my happy place every morning. I walked into the shop and was happy to see my favorite barista, Cori. He is 6'3, with the most amazing tattoo sleeve ever.

Cori said, "Happy Monday, Morgan! I'll have a large caramel macchiato, with an extra shot of espresso, coming right up for you."

I smiled and said, "Thank you, Cori. You always know what I need to get me through my day."

As I was waiting at the end of the counter to pick up my drink, I heard a deep smooth voice from behind me say, "Excuse me, Ms., what drink would you suggest? I usually drink my coffee black, but today I'm in the mood for something different."

I blushed and said, "I would suggest the caramel macchiato or a chai tea."

He smiled with his beautiful white teeth and said to Cori, "I'll have what she's having."

Cori looked at me with a mischievous smile and replied, "What is your name for the drink?"

He said, "Andre."

Cori said, "Ok, Andre, your drink will be up in a minute."

I felt Andre's eyes staring at me, so I asked, "Are you from around here?"

He smiled and said, "No, I'm not. I'm in town at a work conference, so I'll be here for a few days."

I hoped he didn't feel me looking at him, but he had the prettiest smooth dark brown skin, and that smile would brighten anyone's day.

As I walked away, I said, "It was nice to meet you, Andre. Maybe we will bump into each other again here at the coffee shop before you leave town."

Andre cracked half a smile and said, "Let's not leave it to chance."

He took my cell phone out of my hand, added his contact info, handed me back my phone and said, "Now you have it, so make sure you call." Then he turned and walked out of the shop.

The next morning, I called him, and we met at the coffee shop.

He told me he was an electrical engineer, and that he traveled a lot for the company that he worked for. We sat and talked for hours. That was the first time that I felt so connected with someone.

Because Andre traveled so much for his job, we communicated for the most part over Facetime. He would come here to Rhode Island when he could. After doing that for several months, he proposed and moved to Rhode Island with me. I was so happy. 34 years old, and I was finally about to become someone's wife.

---

Detective McKnight said, "Ms. Waters, did Andre tell you where he was living before he moved here?"

Morgan began to fidget in her seat, then said, "He traveled for his job a lot, so he didn't have a permanent residence. He would stay at company-owned homes or a hotel when he was in a city for more than a couple of weeks. Thinking about it now, it was probably all a lie. Looking back on that day, I wish I had never answered Andre when he asked what he should drink...I should have ignored him."

Morgan began rubbing her hands on her lap and biting her lip. She stood up quickly and walked toward the door.

Detective McKnight said, "Ms. Waters, do you need to take a break?"

Exhaling, she said, "Yes, I think I need some time."

"Ok, I have something that I need to take care of. I will come back down here in about 30 minutes, and then you can tell me about the night of your engagement party."

Relieved and happy for the much needed break, Morgan said, "That sounds good."

She folded her arms on the table and laid her head down. Even though she didn't want to, she began to think about that night...

# CHAPTER 5

I twirled around in front of my vanity, admiring how beautiful I looked in my emerald-green gown. I looked over at the clock, and it was approaching time for us to leave.

I yelled from my room, "Andre, please hurry, the car will be here to pick us up to take us to the party in 45 minutes."

Andre scoffed, "Can you stop nagging me? I have a watch; I know what time it is."

I yelled, "I know you have a watch. I bought it like I've bought everything else you are wearing. I've been dreaming of this night for a long time, and I have spent a lot of money. I want everything to be perfect."

Andre had not worked since he moved to Rhode Island to be with Morgan. He went on interviews, but he could never seem to land a job.

Andre slammed his brush down on the dresser and said, "You don't have to remind me that you are the breadwinner every time we have a disagreement. I've been here supporting you the last few months, watching you, while you clawed your way up to partner."

Irritated by his remark, I replied, "Clawed my way up. I worked hard to make partner. Do you know the number of hours and the amount of butt kissing I had to do to make it? It is not easy being a woman in this industry...and a black woman at that."

Andre rolled his eyes and said, "Oh, please stop playing the victim Morgan. You have and always will be ready to do whatever is necessary to get what you want, and you don't care whose lives you ruin to get it."

"Wait...what? Where is that coming from?"

"I don't want to fight, Morgan. This is a special evening...let's just forget it and go."

I said, "We can forget it for now, but we will revisit this conversation at another time."

My phone began to buzz, and I had a text from the driver saying that he was pulling up. I told Andre to hurry up. It was time to leave.

He said, "Morgan, I have to put on my bowtie and cuff links. I'll be down in five minutes"

"Of course, you are never ready on time. I'll meet you in the car."

Andre yelled, "Yeah, I'll see you in the car."

---

Mr. Calloway came to me a few months prior to the engagement party and told me that he and his wife, Jean, wanted to host the party at their home. I was very excited and quickly agreed. I knew that everyone would be talking about my engagement party, and it would be talked about for months at all the social clubs and events, since it would be hosted by the Calloway's at their beautiful home. Any event the Calloway's hosted was always the talk of the town.

Andre and I pulled up to the mansion. I admired the tall, white columns, the beautiful stained-glass windows, and the exquisitely manicured lawn. Andre jokingly asked if we would have to use the back entrance; he said it reminded him of a southern plantation. I rolled my eyes, and we laughed.

He had a way to make me forget how mad I was at him. I always got lost in his eyes. When he put his arms around me, all was right in the world, and I felt secure. That was a feeling I longed for my whole life. Lord knows I didn't have that growing up.

Andre got out of the car, walked over to my car door and opened it. He reached in, and I grabbed his strong bulging arm. As I stepped out of the car, he told me how much he loved me, and how he couldn't take his eyes off of me and all my curves. I was so happy that I had found the perfect dress in such a short period of time, and Andre acknowledging how good I looked in it made me very happy.

We began to walk towards the stairs. I looked at Andre, and he picked me up. He knew just what I was thinking, "*Not in these heels.*" He carried me up the stairs effortlessly, and when we made it to the top, I gave him a kiss, and we entered the mansion.

"Morgan, Andre, welcome to our home." exclaimed Mrs. Calloway.

She is always so bubbly, which is the opposite of Mr. Calloway. She was wearing a long, sequined gold and silver dress, and her hair was pulled up in a bun. It was not my favorite look, but it was an improvement from her usually bland appearance.

Mrs. Calloway said, "We are so happy to host such a beautiful event in our home."

Andre replied, "Thank you, Mrs. Calloway. We could not have dreamed of a more perfect place."

Andre grabbed Mrs. Calloway's hand and kissed it. Mr. Calloway walked up, looking so debonair. He had on a nicely tailored blue Armani suit, a Rolex, and freshly polished Kiton Oxfords.

Mr. Calloway said, "Hey, young man! You are kissing the wrong woman's hand." We all laughed.

The four of us walked out of the corridor towards the guest.

We began to mingle and thank the guests for coming. I had to stop for a moment and take it all in. The luxurious, domed entrance way. The massive, swan ice sculpture—Mr. Calloway has a love for swans. I remember him telling me a story about them before. There were huge, white orchids and bright, oversized chandeliers. The live orchestra played classical music, and I hummed, as I took in the beautifully decorated room. My life was perfect. A handsome, loving fiancé, a beautiful engagement party, and I finally made partner at the firm. Nothing could ruin my perfect evening. At least, that is what I thought.

I looked over and saw Andre talking to a man I'd never seen before. Maybe he knew someone from the firm that I had never met. I don't deal with the staff anymore, unless I need them to do something for me. Either way, the conversation seemed to be getting a little heated, but that could just be Andre. He was very passionate about many things and tended to go a little over the top.

My paralegal, Mya, walked over towards me... "Hi, Mya!"

"Hello, Ms. Waters, thank you again for inviting me. I love your green dress. Where is Andre?"

Rolling my eyes, I said, "Andre? So now you are on a first name basis with him?"

Mya smiled and said, "Sorry if that upsets you. Andre, I mean, Mr. Williams, told me to call him by his first name."

I said, "No worries," as I began to walk away.

I looked up towards the bar to see if Andre was still there, but he was gone, and so was the man he was talking to. My face was sore from smiling at all the guests. I decided to take a break and went to the restroom to freshen up. I was still a bit annoyed by Mya. I didn't work this hard to have my employees call me or my husband by our first names. I think on Monday I will talk with her about my expectations. I went into my little, black sequined bag, grabbed my powder and lipstick, and began to pat my nose and reapply my ruby red lipstick. Red lipstick is not my favorite, but Andre loved it on me.

On my way back into the party, I ran into Mr. Calloway.

He said, "Oh, there you are Morgan! I have been looking all over for you. I hate to do this tonight, but we need to talk strategy on the White case. You know business doesn't stop because you are getting married."

I responded, "Yes, I know. Give me a few minutes to find Andre, and I will meet you in your study."

With a smile on his face Mr. Calloway said, "That's my girl."

I hate when he says that to me. I am a grown woman. I would not dare say that to him, though. I want to keep him happy, because he has mentioned me running the firm when he retires. Mr. and Mrs. Calloway never had children of their own, so they call me their surrogate daughter. I always envisioned my parents being like them.

I walked back into the party looking for Andre, but Mrs. Calloway grabbed my hand and said it was almost time to serve dinner. She would not have anything be off schedule. She was known for her parties, and everything was always perfect. She asked if I had seen Mr. Calloway. I told her he was in his study, and she walked off to get him.

Andre, the man of my dreams, was walking towards me. I couldn't help but to admire him. He had on a white tux and an emerald-green bowtie to match my dress. He filled the tux out nicely. One of the things that attracted me to him was his body. He worked out at least five days a week, faithfully. He leaned down and gave me a kiss. I asked him about the man he was having an intense conversation with at the bar. Andre said that he did not know him. I told him that dinner was about to be served. He held his hand out, I laid my hand into his, and we headed towards the dining area.

When we entered the room, it was so beautiful. It was so warm and cozy. Green and gold cloths draped the tables. Those were our wedding colors. There were large, immaculate flower arrangements on each table. I felt like I was in a room decorated for royalty. Our table was especially exquisite; it was draped in a gold silk cloth with tassels on the ends. On the table, were crystal wine glasses, candles, and rose petals all across it. Behind our plush seats, was an arch that was filled with fresh red roses. It was perfect!

The servers began to bring out the hors d'oeuvres. It was a delicious smoked salmon spread. Andre picked up a cucumber, spread the salmon on it, and took a bite. He said it was as delicious as it looked. I just ate the cucumber—I had become a vegan when I was a child, and I have been one faithfully ever since. I could hear Mr. and Mrs. Calloway laughing with some other attorneys from the firm. Andre's hand was rubbing up and down my back. I smiled and drank some wine. He asked me if I was enjoying the evening, but before I could answer, he leaned over and kissed me on my cheek. Then he stood up and excused himself from the table.

When he left the table, one of the servers came up and reached for his plate. I grabbed it before he could take it, and told him that Andre would be back. As the server was walking away, he handed me a napkin. I looked at him, and he looked over to the man that I saw Andre talking with earlier.

I looked at the man at the table, and he was staring at me with his beady eyes and tacky suit. I wasn't sure if I wanted to open the napkin up. I began to think: *Should I give the napkin to Andre?* The suspicious attorney in me won, and I quickly opened the napkin. It read: *Meet me by the pool near the guest house after the main course. I think you should know who you are about to marry.*

I looked back up and the man was gone. What does he mean, "I should know who I am about to marry?" I know exactly who. The man of my dreams. I noticed Andre walking back to the table, stopping and thanking the guests as he made his way to his seat. I stuck the napkin up under my plate and smiled at Andre, as he sat down next to me.

"Hey, Beautiful, did you miss me?" Andre said with a smile.

I replied, "Of course I did, my love."

Andre picked up his glass and sipped his wine. I watched as he sipped and looked around the room at everyone. I couldn't help to think about the note. Andre has never given me any reason to be suspicious of him. We have our arguments like all couples do, but for the most part, we have a wonderful relationship.

I think the man who had this note delivered to me is crazy. *Why is he here? Who is he? Why would he try to ruin such a perfect evening?* I looked at Andre again. He smiled at me, and all of the questions began to fade away.

As we finished the main course, Mr. Calloway stood up and hit his fork on his crystal wine glass. He said he had a few words that he would like to say. Mr. Calloway had more than his usual amount of alcohol, and as he stood up, he stumbled backwards towards his chair. Jean reached out to help, but he pulled his arm away from her.

He began, "First, I want to thank Morgan and Andre for allowing Jean and I to be a part of this beautiful evening. We never had children of our own. When we met Morgan, fresh out of college, we immediately fell in love with her, and she became part of our family. As the recipient of our scholarship, we proudly watched her start law school as a nervous Tier 1 student to graduate at the top of her class. Morgan is such a driven, dependable, independent, and beautiful young lady. I am honored that she has asked me to walk her down the aisle. Andre, you better take good care of her. I will be watching you. From what I've seen and heard from Morgan and Jean, you are a stand-up guy. Make sure you stay that way. From a man who has been married for over 40 years, here is some advice: Love your wife as you love yourself, listen to her, and always tell her how much you love her."

Jean began to clap, hoping that her husband would get the hint. The guests followed along and began to clap. Then Mr. Calloway sat down.

The servers began to bring out dessert. I hoped that the man was still waiting on me. My curiosity got the best of me. I couldn't marry Andre with this hanging over my head.

I leaned over and whispered in Andre's ear, "I will be right back. I need to go to the restroom." I picked up my purse and gave him a kiss on the forehead. I decided to actually go to restroom, just in case Andre was watching. I peeked out of the door, and the hall was clear, so I took off my heels and darted towards the front door.

I walked outside and put my heels back on—the blistering cold winds hit me in the face. I began to shiver. In my urgent departure from the party, I left my shawl at the table. My nose felt numb as I walked through the dark, somber yard in the bitter cold towards the guest house. I wish I had just gone out the back entrance; it was closer to the guest house. I started to wonder if Andre set this up. Was it a coincidence that I saw them talking earlier at the bar, and then Andre excused himself right before the waiter brought me the napkin? As I was walking, I heard talking. It was heavily muffled and at a distance. It sounded like Andre. I knew he set this up. I wonder if he had something romantic planned. That would not surprise me; Andre always did romantic and spontaneous things. I began to let my guard down, and I sped up my pace and smiled. As I walked towards the pool, my happy demeanor quickly changed. I opened my mouth to scream, but nothing came out.

I couldn't believe what I saw. Andre was standing over the man who I came out to meet, and he had a bloody knife in his hand. The man was on the ground. He looked at me, gasping for air. I ran towards them and pushed Andre out of the way.

I kneeled next to him, and the man said, "Andre is not who you think he is." He made a long piercing gurgling sound and closed his eyes.

I started screaming at Andre and punching him as hard as I could on his chest, "What have you done?"

Andre looked right through me. The hypnotic feeling that I usually got when I looked in his eyes was gone, and now all I saw was emptiness and coldness.

He grabbed me and began to shake me. My body flailed like a swing in the wind.

He said, "Stop yelling! I can explain everything...It was an accident. You have to help me!"

I yanked away from him and said, "Who are you? Who is he? He told me that you are not who I think you are. What does that mean, Andre? What have you done?"

Andre looked at me and said, "I wish you had not said that."

He put his hands around my neck and began to squeeze. His hands became tighter and tighter. I could no longer breathe. Everything began to go dark. I heard some commotion; it must have been people starting to come outside...that's all I remember before I fainted and woke up in the hospital. The doctors told me that he threw me into the pool, and if a good Samaritan hadn't jumped in the water, pulled me out, and performed CPR on me when he did, I would have died.

———

Morgan's heart was beating like a drum and her eyes began to water. She had a throbbing pain in her stomach and a lump in her throat.

The door opened, and Detective McKnight walked into the room. He had been gone for about 30 minutes, and he noticed that she still looked upset. He thought it was because of the questions he had asked earlier—he had no idea she had just relieved the worst night of her life.

Detective McKnight said, "Ms. Waters, you still look very upset. How about we finish this up tomorrow? I have enough information for right now."

She whispered, "Yes, I think that would be best."

Morgan grabbed her coffee mug and purse and ran towards the door. She ran past her police escort. She hated crying in front of people. She felt that people would take that as a sign of weakness.

She began to sprint to her car, because she felt the tears ready to burst from her eyes. She finally made it to her car and began hitting the steering wheel, hoping that the release would postpone the tears that were ready to fall.

It didn't work.

# CHAPTER 6

Detective McKnight went to his office and picked up the phone to call Nita. She was the Forensic tech and a good friend of his. He needed the identity of the victim. Finding out who the victim is would be the first major part of the puzzle into helping him figure out why Andre killed him.

He also knew that he would need some answers for his Captain and District Attorney Hughes soon.

"Hello, Nita," he said.

She exclaimed, "Hey, McKnight! How are you?"

"Nita, you know I'm not calling for small talk. Have you gotten the results back from my victim's DNA?" he replied.

Nita said, "McKnight, you know these things take time. I can't just snap my fingers and the results just appear."

Detective McKnight pulled the phone away from his ear and put his mouth up to the phone and said, "Come on Nita, can you snap your fingers for me?"

"Look, I'll see what I can do. No promises," she said.

"Thanks Nita, I'll call back in the morning for the results." He hung up before she had a chance to reply. He knew Nita would do that for him. After all, he was the one who helped her get the job. She was divorced and in a new city when they met. He knew the right people, and she had the knowledge, along with a winning personality, to get the job.

Detective McKnight began to put all his files in his satchel and headed down to his Captain's office to give an update. The Captain usually let him do his own thing; he was a great detective and always got her results. She tried to partner him up with other detectives, but it never seemed to last. He liked working alone, and he had not disappointed her yet.

He tapped on the Captain's door. She waved him in...she was on the phone, so she put her finger up for Detective McKnight to wait.

After she hung up, she stood and said, "What's up, McKnight?"

He stepped closer to her desk and said, "I just got off the phone with Nita. She will have the identity of our victim soon...at the latest, tomorrow."

She smiled and said, "Good. I was on the phone with District Attorney Hughes when you walked in here, and he was asking for an update. I'll call him back tomorrow then."

Detective McKnight waved and closed the door.

It had been a long day, and he knew that Shelia would not be happy. She wanted to talk, and he had been gone for most of the day. He put on his Kangol and coat and headed towards his car.

# CHAPTER 7

Rhode Island was beautiful in the winter. There was snow, but not too much, like the dark cold winters in the Midwest where Sean was from. He admired the historical buildings downtown. The city was full of culture. The kids could go to museums and walk around. It was a charming town, and that was one of the reasons Sean and Shelia decided to move from their hometown of Ypsilanti, Michigan to Providence, Rhode Island. They agreed that Rhode Island would give them more opportunities, and it would be a wonderful place to raise their kids.

Sean wondered if Shelia had started to prepare dinner. He decided to call her...if she hadn't, he would stop and grab something for the family, to give her a break. "Siri, call Shelia." he said.

The phone rang and rang, but Shelia did not answer. This was not like her; she always picked up. If she was busy, she would say she would call him back. Sean began to think, *Maybe she was still angry about earlier?* He knew one thing for sure, he would find out when he walked through the door.

CHAPTER 7

Sean began to reminiscence on the times when he couldn't wait to walk through those doors, and Shelia would be waiting for him to give him a kiss. Now, she barely looked at him when he came home. For months, when they were not arguing, their conversations did not go any further than what they needed to do for the boys, and what Sean had done wrong.

He had a feeling in the pit of his stomach that something just wasn't right. That's the thing about being a detective for so long... you always think the worse. Maybe Shelia is going to surprise him, like she used to, with a quiet evening and no boys, so they could talk?

As he pulled up, he saw Ms. Parker. She is the neighbor who knows everything that is going on in the neighborhood. If she didn't know, she would make up her own version and swear by her story. Sean wasn't in the mood to entertain her. He decided that he would have a very brief exchange of customary greetings and quickly make his way to the front door.

"Hello, Ms. Parker."

Lifting her head up, like she didn't notice the car pulling in she said, "Hello, Sean. I thought you would be with Shelia unpacking the moving truck."

Sean looked at her confused. She said, "Yes, the movers were here earlier, and Shelia said that you all were moving across town."

Sean turned quickly and ran towards the front door. He was fidgeting badly with the keys in the lock, because his hands were shaking. He could barely open the door, and when he was finally able to open it, he walked inside, and fell to his knees. His worst nightmare had come true...Shelia and the boys were gone.

He looked around the empty space, and a dreadful feeling came over him. As he scanned the room, the only thing that was left in the living room, was a picture of the boys, and his dirty old brown recliner that had the worn-out arm rest.

Sean ran up the stairs, having to catch himself, as he skipped over several stairs. He ran to the boys' room, opened the door, and

30

their beds were gone. Sean ran back down the stairs. He was angry and out of breath. How could Shelia do this? Just move and take the boys, without even a discussion. When did she start packing their things? What did he miss? The Shelia that Sean married would never do anything like this! Does she hate him so much that she would take his kids?

He grabbed his phone and began frantically dialing her number. He held the back of his head and walked back and forth. No answer. He hung up and called again...he walked into the kitchen, and on the counter, was a white envelope. On the outside it said, *Goodbye Sean*. He hung up the phone, and his hands began to shake uncontrollably...they were shaking so violently, that he could not open the letter. He sat down on the floor, because his knees began to buckle. He wanted to get up and get a glass of water because his mouth felt like cotton, but he couldn't move.

Sean prepared himself for what he was about to read. He bowed his head and said a quick prayer. His hands became steady, and then he opened the letter.

*Dear Sean,*

*I am sorry to leave this way, but I cannot do this anymore. You promised that the boys and I would always come first. But we have taken a back seat to your career. Emotionally, we have not been a couple for years. I am tired of feeling like I have a roommate and not a husband. I told you that I wanted to see a therapist to work on our relationship, but you were always too busy.*

*You are a wonderful father and detective, but a horrible husband. I can't continue to live like this any longer. You promised me this would never happen again. You promised me that you would never be consumed with this job like you were with your first case, solving the murder of your high school sweetheart. I'm tired of being second place to your job, Sean.*

*Please do not contact me. I will send you an email with the boy's schedule, so that we can work out times for you to see them. I hired a lawyer, and she is drafting divorce papers. I love you, Sean, but I am*

*no longer in love with you. I want someone in my life who puts me first. Please do not fight this. I am done!!*
   *Shelia*


Sean's tears began to soak the paper, so much so, that Shelia's writing had become illegible. It had now become a big blue stain on a piece of paper. He had not been alone in the home they bought together since they were first married—before the boys—when Shelia went to visit her mother back in Michigan for a week. He couldn't imagine coming home every day with his boys not being there, looking out the windows, waiting on him. He decided it would be best to give Shelia some space and wait until the morning to call her again.

He, finally, was able to get himself off the floor. With his head hanging, he headed towards the bathroom to wash his face and to gather his composure. As he walked through the empty, quiet halls, he was reminded that he had lost his family. He looked at the bathroom, but did not have the energy to enter. He decided the best thing for him was to go to sleep for the night.

# CHAPTER 8

Detective McKnight's mind was all over the place. He lay in the bed, staring at the ceiling, when he was startled by the vibration of his phone on his nightstand. He squinted at the alarm clock; it was 7:00 a.m. He picked up the phone, hoping it was Shelia saying she came back to her senses and was coming home. He sighed, when he realized that it was not Shelia, but a text from Sergeant Paddington. It read, *There is a young lady here who says she has some information about Morgan Waters that you need to hear.*

Detective McKnight replied, "Tell her I will be there in 30 minutes."

He jumped out of bed and decided against a shower; he had no time. He grabbed the closest suit in his closet, which was not like him. He put great pride into how he looked. He hurried down the stairs, picked up the picture of his boys, and gave it a kiss. Then he grabbed his keys, turned and looked at his empty house, and headed towards his car.

He was in a complete fog the whole drive into the station. This morning was so much different than any morning he had in years.

No kids screaming, no breakfast cooking, and no *I love you, Daddy*, before he walked out of the door. He remembered getting into the car, and the next thing he knew, he was pulling into his parking space at the police station.

Paddington greeted him with a smile as he walked in. He said that he sat the woman in the conference room, and that she was very upset and had been crying since she arrived. Detective McKnight began to walk down the hall...he decided to stop by the break room and grab a cup of coffee, to make it through the conversation. He had walked down those halls thousands of times, usually with confidence, energy, and swag. However, this time, the halls seemed rather long, and his legs felt like bricks. What usually would have been a five-minute walk, now felt like a 20 minute one. He finally made it to the conference room. He reached out to open the door, trying to balance the cup of coffee, a notepad, and a pen. He was unsuccessful, as the steamy coffee spilled on his finger. He shook his hand, hoping that the stinging would stop, then opened the door and saw, sitting there, a frail young lady, with stringy hair. She had on a red and black long-sleeved fleece and torn jeans. She also reeked of cigarette smoke.

He sat everything down on the table, reached out his hand, and said, "Hello, I am Detective McKnight."

She reached out her cold, clammy hands and shook his saying, "My name is Robin Harris, and I have information for you about Morgan Waters."

As Detective McKnight sat in the interview room in front of Ms. Harris, he became very curious. Who is this lady? What is her motivation to be here? Who is she to Ms. Waters? And what information could she give that can help me solve this case? What does she have that is so important that she could not just call?

Detective McKnight leaned forward, grabbed his pen and notepad, and said, "Ms. Harris, I appreciate you contacting this office. May I ask how you heard about this murder? From what I understand, you are not from this city."

Robin Harris looked up at Detective McKnight with her glossy eyes and said, "My mother is friends with Morgan's aunt, and she told me what supposedly happened." She put her hands up over her eyes and said, "You cannot believe anything that Morgan tells you. She is a liar and a murderer. She killed our best friend in college and got away with it."

Ms. Harris began to cry and asked for a tissue. Detective McKnight reached for the box beside him, pulled out a few, and handed them to her.

It took a few minutes for her to gain her composure. Every time she tried to talk, tears began to fall, and she would choke over her words.

Detective McKnight asked, "Would you like a bottle of water?"

She replied, "Yes."

While he was walking out of the room to grab Ms. Harris a bottle of water, his phone began to ring. He looked down, and it was Shelia. He exhaled and continued to walk towards the break room. He decided not to answer, because he was in the middle of an interview, and he could not deal with whatever Shelia wanted to say at that moment. She had a gift of calling and texting him when he was busy.

Detective McKnight heard a buzz, and there was a voicemail notification on his phone. He began to loosen his tie and unbutton the first two buttons of his shirt. He felt like his airway was constricted. He moved his head from side to side, as he held his hand between his neck and his shirt. He was conflicted: could Shelia be calling because there was some emergency with the boys, or was she calling to fight? He knew her, and if it was an emergency, she would call his phone until he picked up...and if that didn't work, she would call the front desk, and have Sergeant Paddington hunt him down. Detective McKnight took a deep breath, fixed his tie and shirt, and went back into the conference room.

Robin Harris was sitting there biting her nails. When he

walked in, she said, "Sorry, I always bite my nails when I am nervous."

Detective McKnight handed her the water and said, "This room has that effect on some people, but I can assure you, Ms. Harris, you have no reason to be nervous here. As long as you are completely honest with me. Please, take a deep breath and relax."

Robin began, "Detective McKnight, you need to understand. Morgan will do anything to keep this perfect image of herself and to make her dreams come true. She will eliminate anyone or anything that gets in her way. I have known her since kindergarten. It hurts to say these things about her because she was like a sister to me, but I can't stand by and let her ruin any more lives."

Leaning back in his chair, Detective McKnight said, "Those are some pretty strong allegations, Ms. Harris, do you have any proof to back up your story?"

She sighed, "No, I do not have any physical evidence, but I was there, and I know what happened."

Ms. Harris began to breathe very hard, and she reached for her old, scratched up, blue purse. She took a bottle of pills out, quickly popped two in her mouth, and drank water behind them.

"What do you mean you were there?" replied Detective McKnight.

Robin's knees began to bounce, and they hit the underside of the table like a drum. She said, "I was not actually there to see her kill our friend, Shawna. What I do know, is that I talked to both Morgan and Shawna that day, and they had gotten into a huge argument. Shawna called me crying, and said she had never seen Morgan so angry. She asked me if she could stay at my dorm for the night, to give Morgan some time to calm down. I told her, yes. Two hours later, I received a frantic phone call from Morgan. She was screaming on the phone, and she told me that Shawna was dead. She said it was her fault that she killed her. When I got there and asked her what happened, she said that Shawna had died by suicide. I asked her what Morgan meant when she said on the phone it was her fault that she killed Shawna. She said that she meant the argument was what drove Shawna to kill herself. I didn't believe her then, and if I were you, I wouldn't believe anything she is telling you now."

The room was silent. Detective McKnight began to scratch his head. He began to write on his notepad. *If this story is true, I would definitely need to look at Ms. Waters closer. Maybe she is more than the innocent victim that she portrayed. Morgan Waters=Victim????*

Robin said, "Detective, I am begging you. Please do not let Morgan get away with two murders."

Detective McKnight escorted Robin Harris to the front of the station. He thanked her for sharing the information, pulled out his pen, and wrote down how to contact her, just in case he had any more questions. She said goodbye and left the building. His phone began to ring again...he yanked it out of his pocket and prepared himself for a fight with Shelia, but he looked down, and it was District Attorney Frank Hughes.

Detective McKnight put his phone back into his pocket, but then pulled it back out, debating on if was going to answer it, or if he would let it go to voicemail. He had not even brought his Captain up to date on the new developments, and he surely wasn't in the mood for all of the district attorney's questions. He still needed to process the information that Robin Harris had just given him.

Before the last ring, Detective McKnight answered, "Hello, Frank."

He replied, "Hi, Sean, I'm calling regarding the Andre Williams murder case. Have you made any progress?"

Detective McKnight began to rub his eyebrows, feeling a headache coming on. He replied, "The case was just given to me a couple of days ago. We are still in the early stages. I'm waiting to hear back from the forensic lab to find out who our victim is, and I am conducting interviews. I have nothing for you at this moment."

District Attorney Hughes said, "Ok, Sean, keep me posted. I'm getting a lot of pressure about this one. As you know, Ms. Waters works for one of the most influential attorneys in the state, and this murder happened at his house. He has a lot of friends, and he has called all of them. Now they are calling me. We need this to be quick and clean."

"I'll call you when I have more information." Detective McKnight hung up before District Attorney Hughes could reply.

That's the thing Detective McKnight hated about the district attorney's office: they expected top notch evidence and witnesses, and wanted you to have it in a short period of time, which is unreasonable. Detective McKnight has never really liked District Attorney Frank Hughes. They bumped into each other at a few social gatherings and played a few games of pick-up basketball. The district attorney was two inches taller than Detective McKnight, and he was all muscle. Most of the time, the spectators at the pick-up game were all women cheering Frank on.

Detective McKnight had so many things whirling through his head at the speed of light. Could he have been fooled by Ms. Waters' big brown eyes and stunning smile? Could she be a cold-blooded killer?

His phone pinged; he had a text from Shelia. He threw his head back, put his hand on his forehead, and thought *I cannot believe I forgot to call her back.* He looked at the text, and it said, *"The boys tried to call you earlier, but of course you didn't pick up. They wanted to say good morning, but they are at school now. I need to know if you can swing by my apartment tomorrow morning and drop them to school...I have an appointment with the divorce attorney. My address is 2708 Ainsworth.*

He reread the message, because he couldn't believe that she hadn't even mentioned the fact that she just upped and left. Pressing the keys as hard and quickly as he could, he responded, "Unfortunately, Shelia, I have an appointment in the morning. I think it is very selfish and rude that you left without talking to me.

This is truly sad that after all we have been through we are now communicating by text."

Detective McKnight watched the clock as time went by. Shelia never responded. That's how she has always handled things when the conversation got tough; she always went silent.

He needed to clear his mind, so he pulled out the gym bag that he kept in his office and grabbed some clothes and his running shoes. Running usually helped him to put things into perspective. He started down the trail from the police station—it took him through downtown and to the park—after running for about two miles, he wiped the little snowflakes off of a bench and sat down.

He couldn't get the conversation he had with Robin Harris off his mind. The snow started to come down harder, so he got up and ran back to the station.

# CHAPTER 9

The run was exactly what Sean needed, and he was finally able to get a good night's rest. He reached for the alarm clock that had been going off for the last 15 minutes. He hit the button to stop it and grabbed his phone; there was still no reply from Shelia. As he began to roll out of bed, his phone rang. It was Nita!

"Good morning, Nita." he said, as he sat on the edge of the bed.

"Good morning, Sean. I have the identity of the victim. His name is Johnathan Grey, and he is a private investigator from Tennessee," she exclaimed.

Detective McKnight was now standing. Excited by the news, he said, "Nita, you are the sunshine of my life. Thank you! I owe you. When this case is over, I'm going to take you out for your favorite steak and scotch...on me."

Nita chuckled and said, "Sounds good, Sean. Just a heads-up, District Attorney Hughes called my office this morning, and he left a voicemail asking if I had any information on the victim. I have not called him back yet."

Sighing, Sean said, "All the higher-ups are putting a lot of pressure on District Attorney Hughes, so he is putting pressure on me. A prominent lawyer's fiancé is the suspect in this murder, and he also tried to kill her, *and* this all happened at the home of one of the most influential attorneys in Providence. Thanks for the heads-up. I will contact the district attorney to bring him up to date, and I'll be talking to you soon."

Detective McKnight began to scratch his head. This case is becoming stranger by the minute. Why was a private investigator from Tennessee here following Andre? He decided to call Morgan Waters to see if the name, Johnathan Grey, sounded familiar.

Sean reached over onto his dusty nightstand and grabbed his notepad. It had not been cleaned since before Shelia left; she would usually clean the rooms on Saturdays. He began to flip through the pages and found Morgan Waters' phone number...he picked up his phone and called.

"Good morning, Ms. Waters, this is Detective McKnight. How are you?"

She replied, "I'm fine. I'm hoping to go back to work today. It has been a few days and Andre has not tried anything. Do you really think it is necessary for me to still have a police officer following me? I'm ready to get back to my life, and that does not include being shadowed by an officer."

Detective McKnight said, "Ma'am, we have made some progress in the case, and hopefully it will help us catch Andre...but I would feel more comfortable if we kept the officer there for a few more days."

Morgan let out a huge sigh and said, "I guess that's best."

"I do have a few questions for you. Have you ever heard Mr. Williams mention the name Johnathan Grey?"

Morgan began to look up at the ceiling and twirled the one last curl she had left in her hair and said, "A few weeks ago, Andre did receive some mail from him. I remember, because he quickly took it from my hand...and when I asked who that was, he said it was an old friend he hadn't talked to in years. Then I asked him, if he hadn't talked to this friend in years, how did he know where we lived? Andre said that he probably found it through social media. I thought it was strange, but I didn't think anything else of it."

Intrigued about the letter, Detective McKnight asked, "Do you know what he did with the letter?"

Annoyed by the questions Morgan scoffed, "No, I don't. I put all of his things in boxes and stuck them in the basement. I didn't know what else to do with them. Feel free to come and get them, look through them, burn them. I really don't care; I just want you to find him, so I can have my life back."

He said, "Great!! I will be over with a warrant. I also would like to ask you a few questions about Robin Harris and Shawna Smith."

She whispered, "What? Robin and Shawna?"

"Ms. Waters, are you there?" he said.

"Yes! What does this have to do with them?" Morgan protested.

"To be honest, I am not sure...but Robin Harris came and visited me yesterday, and she had some very disturbing things to say about you, and I need some answers from you."

———

Morgan began to clench and unclench her fist. She bit down on her lip so hard that she began to taste blood. She started tapping her fingers on the table, wondering how much Robin had told Detective McKnight.

As a seasoned attorney, she was well aware of the sneaky tactics the police used to get people to talk more than they should. She knew that Robin was not the same strong young lady that she once considered a sister. Robin had been addicted to drugs for years. She was in and out of rehab more times than anyone could count. Robin's mother had blown through her entire retirement putting Robin into different rehab facilities. Now, to supplement her income, her mother is a greeter at Walmart.

Morgan went and picked up her phone, and she saw that she had a missed call from Mr. Calloway; he left a voicemail:

"Hello, Morgan, this is Mr. Calloway here. Jean told me you talked, and you are planning to come into work today. I know that you are ambitious and a very hard worker, but I am worried about you. You just went through a very traumatic experience, and I think that you should take a few more days. I can give some of your cases to a couple of the junior associates...that'll give them something to do. Call me back, and let me know what you want to do. I hope you think about what I said. Talk to you soon."

Morgan needed to be at work busy. Her work was everything to her. She always dreamed of being a lawyer, and that came first. Andre had taken away so much from her, and she was not going to let him take her career away from her too. Morgan called Mr. Calloway back, and she let him know that under no circumstance was he to give any of her cases to a junior associate. She would definitely be going into work.

She went downstairs and poured her coffee.

Morgan was staring outside, looking at her birdhouse. She was always mesmerized by the hummingbird. It was tiny, but determined...and the way it changed direction so quickly, was amazing.

Morgan decided she had to get ahead of the Robin Harris issue. She opened her laptop and started searching Delta for flights to Michigan.

# CHAPTER 10

Detective McKnight started to knock on the office door of District Attorney Frank Hughes.

"Come in!" District Attorney Hughes exclaimed.

Detective McKnight walked in. He couldn't help but to see all of the plaques and awards covering the walls in the office, and right in the middle of them all—right over District Attorney Hughes' head, in a huge frame—was his Juris Doctor from the University of Harvard.

District Attorney Hughes stood up and said, "Hi, Sean, please have a seat. I hope you are here with an update on the murder."

Sean took a deep breath, sat down, and said, "There have been quite a few developments today. I found out from the forensic team the identity of the victim; his name is Johnathan Grey, and he was a private investigator from Tennessee."

Sean leaned over and handed Frank a folder with all the information from the forensic specialist and the autopsy. He had stopped to see Nita and the medical examiner on his way to the district attorney's office.

Frank began to look through the paperwork. A frown came over his face, and he said, "This was a vicious attack. He stabbed the private investigator at least 20 times. Sean, we have to get this guy off the street. He is a danger to anyone who comes into contact with him. He is a cold-blooded killer!"

Nodding his head in agreement, Sean said, "Yes, he is, and I am working on it. I talked to Ms. Waters this morning, and she told me that she remembered a letter that Andre Williams received from Johnathan Grey. She gave me permission to go through the boxes that she put all of Andre's things in, but I thought it would be best to come and get a warrant. When we catch him, I don't want any evidence being tossed on a technicality."

Frank opened his drawer, pulled out a form, and grabbed his pen. He filled out the search warrant, then called up a judge and faxed the warrant over to her to be signed. Ten minutes later, the warrant was being faxed back over. The DA grabbed it and handed it to Detective McKnight.

Sean thanked Frank, and then got on his phone and called his Captain. He told her that a judge had signed a search warrant, and he needed a couple of patrolmen to meet him at Ms. Waters' residence to take the boxes to the police station.

---

There was a rumble on the table. It startled Morgan, and she knocked over the little bit of coffee left in her cup. She ran over and grabbed a paper towel, and began to clean up the mess. There was a rumble again. Her phone does that to notify her when there is someone at her door. She looked at the camera, and it was Detective McKnight, with two other officers.

She couldn't believe she had sat there and lost track of time. She hit the speaker button on her phone, and told him she would be with them in a moment.

Morgan was still in her red robe; she ran upstairs and found a red scrunchie to pull her hair back. She put on her yoga pants and her oversized Ohio State sweatshirt. She stepped into her UGG slippers and ran back to the door. When she finally made it there, she was out of breath.

She said, "Hello, Detective McKnight"

He replied, "Hello. These officers are here to help bring Andre's things to the police station."

She hurried them in as the cold air blew past them into her living room, leaving an appearance of crystals over her screen door. It was unusually cold for the beginning of December; it usually didn't get this cold until the end of January, or early February.

Detective McKnight began to take off his gloves and rubbed his hands together. He said, "It's pretty nippy outside today."

Morgan said, "Would you all like coffee or hot chocolate?"

They all declined and Detective McKnight asked Morgan to lead them to her basement. They entered the basement, and in a far corner in the back, sat a mountain of boxes neatly stacked with Andre's name on them.

Morgan said, "There you go. You can have at them. All of his things have his name marked on them."

Detective McKnight said, "Thank you, Morgan" and then he turned to the patrolmen and said with a grin, "Can you please take the boxes to the station and put them in my office? I would help, but I'm healing from an old injury."

One of the patrolmen said, "Sean, that excuse is getting old." They chuckled and headed toward the boxes.

Detective McKnight and Morgan walked back upstairs, because he still needed answers regarding his conversation with Robin Harris. They walked through the kitchen and into the living room.

He said, "I know that you have been through a lot these past few days, but I have to ask...why would Robin Harris accuse you of murdering your friend, Shawna Smith, when you all were in college?"

Morgan's knees felt weak, her face became hot, and sweat was pouring down her cheeks. Her heart was beating 500 beats a minute. She became very dizzy and fell back onto her sofa.

Detective McKnight said, "Morgan! Morgan! Ms. Waters, are you ok...do you need to go to the hospital?"

She looked up at him, and tears were streaming from her face; they met the snot outside of her nose, and both were running onto her lip. Detective McKnight handed her a piece of tissue that he had in his coat pocket. She reached out and reluctantly grabbed it. She never cried in front of people, but at that moment, she didn't care. She wasn't sure if it was overwhelming sadness, the guilt that she carried for so many years, or the idea that all her darkest secrets were about to come out.

Morgan's sadness quickly turned into rage. She grabbed her yellow, decorative pillow with the blue, red, and green parrot. She buried her face in it and started to scream.

Detective McKnight reached over and grabbed her shoulder and said, "Ms. Waters, it's ok...whatever it is, you can tell me—I can help you."

Morgan looked up and said, "I am a horrible person. Everything Andre did to me, I deserved. It is my fault that Shawna died in college, and it's my fault that the private investigator was outside when Andre murdered him. He was there to meet me."

Detective McKnight could not believe what he just heard. He said, "So, what are you trying to tell me, Ms. Waters? You murdered your friend, *and* you had Andre murder Johnathan Grey at the engagement party?"

Morgan stood up and said, "NO! I would never murder anyone or have anyone murdered. I made a lot of bad mistakes that caused a lot of pain and misery for others. I knew that one day it would all come back to bite me. I never imagined that it would be like this. Before I say anything else. I would like to call a lawyer."

Detective McKnight said, "Ok, you do that...and I'll need you and your attorney to come down to the station as soon as possible."

# CHAPTER 11

S ean loved driving through the older neighborhoods in Providence; there were so many historical homes and sites. On the rare occasion that he had a weekend off, Sean, Shelia, and the boys would take long walks through the neighborhoods and read the plaques in the yards that gave the history of each home. Sean wanted to call Shelia, but it was 2:00 p.m., and the boys were still in school. She made it clear that she didn't want any communication with him unless it was regarding the boys.

When Detective McKnight walked into the police station, he was greeted by Sergeant Paddington, who said with a smile, "I saw all the boxes being brought to your office, McKnight. Shelia finally tossed your behind out, huh?"

Detective McKnight returned a quick smirk. Paddington had no idea how close he was to the truth. Those words stabbed Sean deeply. He went into his office, where he could no longer hold back the tears. He wiped his eyes, and then looked at the pile of boxes. Walking over, he took down the first box and began going through it. The box was marked, *Miscellaneous*. He was hoping that he would open the first box, and the letter would be sitting right on top, but of course that did not happen.

He contemplated having someone help him go through the boxes, but he changed his mind...he needed the distraction to keep his mind off of Shelia and the boys.

There was a knock on detective McKnight's door. The Captain stepped in and told him the officer assigned to escort Ms. Waters had been trying to get into contact with him. He said there was a light blue van that drove by the house a couple of times. The windows were tinted, so he was unable to see the driver, but he was able to get the plates. He had called it in, and the car was reported stolen yesterday.

Detective McKnight said, "Maybe we should beef up her security?"

The Captain gave a thumbs up and said, "It's already done, McKnight. I added two extra officers, and I had a BOLO put out on the car. If that was, in fact, Andre Williams, we will get him."

---

Morgan's mind was moving 100 miles a minute. Who should she call? Mr. Calloway is the best attorney that she knew, but what will he think about her when he finds out the truth? She wanted to call her mother, because her mom would know exactly what she should do. Morgan missed her mother very much. Not a day went by that she didn't think of her. It is cruel what happens when you lose your mother at such a young age. She didn't have her to go to for advice; to cry to when it seemed like the whole world was against her; to vent to about her boyfriends, boss, or colleagues. If she was there, maybe Morgan would not have made the bad decisions that she did. Maybe her mother would have seen right through Andre's charm and warned her to stay away, then maybe that summer before college would have never happened.

Morgan stared at the owl clock on her wall. Slowly, the big

hand clicked, as it moved methodically around the dial—every fifteen minutes, his eyes would move; and at the top of the hour, he would hoot. As she sat there, there was a feeling of a bowling ball in her stomach. She knew she was about to have to do one of the hardest things ever in her life. Confess her sins.

Morgan decided to call Mr. Calloway. There was no one who she trusted more, and she knew that he would relentlessly defend her. She was also well aware of the fact that he had many connections, and those connections could only help her. She called Mr. Calloway and briefly caught him up on what was going on. Then she asked if he could represent her, and told him that she would go into more detail when they met.

---

Mrs. Calloway opened her door, and there was Morgan. She held her arm out motioning Morgan to come in. She gave Morgan a hug and said, "Morgan, we have been so worried about you. How are you?"

Even though she was not being honest, Morgan reassured Mrs. Calloway that she was ok, and that she had no reason to worry.

Mrs. Calloway continued, "Henry told me that he called you earlier and left you a message. I know you are here to talk to him. He just stepped out for a few minutes. I'll take you to his study if you would like, and you can wait on him there."

"That would be nice. Thank you!"

Morgan sat in Mr. Calloway's study and waited for him to return home. She always loved his study with the beautiful high ceilings. The dark, wooden shelves were home to thousands of books: he had legal ones, self-help, how-to, novels, and poems...more books than she could ever imagine reading. Mr. Calloway told her that he had read every single one of them. The dark wood was accented by beautiful, burgundy Persian rugs and big brown leather chairs. Mr. Calloway had beautiful pieces of art spread perfectly throughout the room. Morgan's favorite seat was the brown leather chaise lounge with gold buttons, that closely followed the trim. It sat right next to a huge bay window. That spot was her serenity—it looked like a paradise. There were trees and perfectly manicured grass. She would see deer, rabbits, ducks, and every once in a while, a beautiful swan would come and grace the pond.

Her favorite things to look at were the red oak trees. The majestic branches looked like they were reaching towards the sky. The leaves were simple: green, shiny, and elliptical shaped, but the magnificence of the tree was shown best in the fall. The green leaves turned a bright red, with a gold trim. It exuded endurance, strength, and longevity. But even that tree today was barren, dark, and snow-covered.

Morgan could relate to the tree. She was always reaching toward the sky, and although she loved the finer things in life, she was still that simple little girl, who at times just wanted her mom. Even though she always tried to shine brightly, she experienced times of darkness, coldness, and emptiness.

Morgan jumped, as Mr. Calloway walked into the room carrying his black briefcase, that had a dent in the left corner. He put it down on his desk, fidgeted with the lock on the side of it, and opened it up. He pulled out a legal-sized notepad and a pen. Mr. Calloway looked at Morgan with somber, concerned eyes and said, "Morgan, I need you to start from the beginning, and do not leave anything out. The only way that I can help you, is if I know the complete story. I want you to start with what happened the summer before you went to college."

Morgan looked at Mr. Calloway and then peered out the window. She took a deep breath and started to snap the pink breast cancer awareness band that she always wore on her wrist in remembrance of her mom. Snapping the band on her arm is just one of the many tools she had learned over the years from her therapist on how to deal with anxiety and the feeling of being overwhelmed.

She stood up and began to pace the room, as if she was about to give an opening statement to a jury. Morgan stopped and looked at Mr. Calloway then said, "I hope that after you hear what I have to say, that you and Jean will still love me and allow me to be a part of your life. You are all the family that I have. I have never been able to count on my worthless father. I am sorry if what I am about to tell you disappoints you. I never wanted any of this to happen. I never thought it would go this far..."

# CHAPTER 12

I t was the summer of 2005. Robin, Shawna, and I decided that we would take a road trip before we started college. Shawna and I were going to be roommates at Ohio State University. I had received a scholarship for a full ride, and Shawna's parents were alumni, so she was automatically accepted. Robin was going to attend Franklin University, which was a college eight minutes away from OSU.

We packed up my midnight blue, 2002 Toyota Camry—the one gift that my dad gave me—and left Ohio, heading south. We decided that we would go to North Carolina, Georgia, Alabama, and our final destination was Florida. We were so excited; this trip would be our introduction into adulthood. This was especially exciting for Shawna, because her parents were extremely strict and never let her do anything. This would be her first trip without them.

Robin and I pulled up at Shawna's, and she ran out of the front door, as if she was the anchor leg in a track race. She had one bag with her: it was an old, beat- up, green suitcase with a *Peace* sign on it. She threw her bag on the back seat, hopped in the car, and yelled, "GO!"

Robin asked Shawna why she ran out of the house like she was Jackie Joyner Kersey. Shawna confessed to us that she had not told her parents about the road trip. Instead, she had left a letter on the kitchen table, and she wanted to leave before they came home and were able to read it. We sat in silence for about 30 seconds, and then we started to laugh hysterically. Shawna reached to the front, turned the radio to 97.9 WJLB, and we started to sing along with Usher.

We finally made it through Ohio; which seemed like it took forever. We pulled over at a rest stop to take a nap, instead of wasting money at a hotel. We took turns napping, so that there was always someone awake to watch for danger. We rested for a bit and then drove into Kentucky. We stopped and had breakfast at this small diner. I think the name was Charlie's Diner, but the bulbs in the 'C' had blown out. We saw an empty booth in the back, and we sat there. The diner had black-and-white checker floors and red pleather benches. The booth had a red seat and a rip down the middle. Shawna stepped outside of the restaurant to call her parents and let them know that she was ok. When she came back into the diner, her eyes were red, and she laid her head down on the table and said she didn't want anything to eat.

After we left the restaurant, we went to the gas station up the street and filled up.

I reluctantly handed the keys over to Robin to drive. I had never let anyone drive my car. My eyes were tired, and I needed a break. Besides, Robin was a seasoned driver, and she had driven through the mountains before. It was just Robin and her mother. Every summer they would go on long road trips. When Robin was able to drive, her mom would let her take over for a few hours, so that she could get some rest.

Robin drove longer than I expected, but I was happy, because that meant I could continue to sleep. We decided to go to a rest stop right before we entered Tennessee. We all jumped out of the car and ran into the bathroom. I hated using rest-stop bathrooms. There were 10 stalls but only about two were fit to use. There was toilet paper all over the floor and you had to search for a dispenser that had soap.

I often wondered, if we had not made that stop, maybe things would have been different. It was Shawna's turn to drive. She hopped in the driver seat and was going to drive for maybe an hour, depending on how it went. Shawna was the worst driver out of the three of us. We jumped on US-11W N. Shawna turned up the radio, and we began to sing, "One, Two, Step," with Ciara. The next thing we knew, Shawna had been driving for two hours; so, we decided to let her continue. We pulled over to grab some snacks. I grabbed a Coke and BBQ chips, Robin had an array of candy, and Shawna finally decided to grab some sunflower seeds. Robin and I stood at the cash register waiting for Shawna; we laughed, because we knew she would end up with the sunflower seeds...that's what she always got.

Shawna started to drive down a dark road heading back towards the highway. We were laughing, singing, and snacking. That's when we heard it. There was a thump, and it felt like we drove over a speed bump. I turned around to look and saw something lying in the road. I yelled to Shawna to stop and back up. We got out of the car, and that's when we saw it. It was not a deer or a speed bump. It was a young man; he had on jeans and a blue and white striped shirt...and because of us, the shirt had a huge red spot that continued to spread all over it. In his hand, was a brown bag and some keys. On the ground next to him, was a cell phone and an open bag of Funyuns. We began to scream, then Robin reached down and checked his pulse. He was dead.

My hands were shaking uncontrollably. Shawna was screaming, and Robin was trying to console her. Shawna said that we should call the police. I went for my phone, and Robin ripped it from my hand.

Robin said, "Look, we don't know where we are. We don't know if he was already in the road dead, and we just ran over him. What I do know, is that if we call the police, we can go to jail. Do you want to be in jail in some place like this, far away from home?"

I replied, "No, but we can't just leave him like a dead animal in the road."

Shawna yelled, "What are you all thinking? We have to call the police!"

Robin took a deep breath and said, "Shawna you were driving, we are trying to protect you."

I knew we had to do something, but I also knew Robin was right. At that moment, all I could think of was losing my scholarship... all my hard work would be for nothing. I suggested we go up the street and call the police from the pay phone. If we called from my cell phone, the police would be able to track the call back to me.

Shawna screamed, "We can't just leave him in the street!"

There was a ditch next to him, so we decided to put him in it so no one else would run over him.

I grabbed his arms, and Shawna and Robin grabbed his legs. My foot became stuck in some mud on the side of the road— it had rained earlier. I began to slip, but regained my footing. I told the girls that on the count of three, we would toss him in the ditch. *1, 2, 3...* We threw him; it was like carrying a ton of bricks. He was so heavy. When I looked down, all I saw looking back up at me were the most piercing blue eyes. As I looked in his eyes, I wondered who would be missing him. A lump grew in my throat, my chest began to hurt, so I turned away.

I got in the driver's side of the car and drove up the street until we found a pay phone. I got out, called the police, and told them that a body was in a ditch on the service drive. The next few hours in the car was silent. Shawna once again suggested that we turn around and go home, but Robin and I were both adamant that we were going to finish our trip. Besides, it was too late—we were at the point of no return...we left a dead body in a ditch beside the road. What was done was done.

Two weeks later, we returned home. I was never so excited to be back in Ohio. We had all decided that we would never bring up what happened again. We started college, and the best part of school was that Shawna and I were roommates. The worse part, was seeing her struggle day after day with what happened. For some reason, I was able to keep going. I convinced myself of the fact that because we didn't see him walking across the street, that he was already dead on the road.

One day, I came to the dorm after taking a nerve-wracking physics test. Shawna was balled up in the corner of her bed. Her head was laying against the wall, on her Usher poster. She was pale and had a wet tissue in her hand. When I got closer, I noticed that she was shivering, and her mascara had stained her face. I asked her what was wrong, and she began to shake her head.

She turned her computer towards me. My heart stopped, and I ran to the bathroom and threw up. It was a news article from a Tennessee crime blog and the headline said, "Three months later, and the hit and run murder of young athlete still unsolved." I ran back over to Shawna and turned off the computer. She grabbed her phone, called Robin, and told her she needed to come to our dorm now.

Robin arrived, and Shawna showed her the article. Robin asked her why she was looking at the newspaper from Tennessee. We were supposed to have acted like the accident never happened. Robin began to panic.

Shawna said, "I wanted to call the police from the beginning, and you two would not let me. I have not had a decent night sleep since this all happened. Every night, I see that boy lying in the street covered in blood—last night I looked at his face, but it was Eli. I saw my brother lying there in the street, dead. What if that *was* my brother or someone else we knew or loved? We just left him there, like an animal."

Shawna's eyes were overflowing with tears, and she said that she could no longer keep our secret—she was going to confess. She said that the truth was going to come out anyway. I told her she could not do that—it would ruin our lives. I wanted to go to law school. Even if we didn't go to jail, I would never be able to be an attorney, if that was on my record. Shawna said she didn't care.

I began to heat up on the inside...all I could do was see my future slipping away. I yelled at her and told her she couldn't ruin our lives because she had a guilty conscious. We sat in the room for hours; it was so quiet, that you could hear a pin drop.

Then I said, "Look, we cannot change what happened. Do I wish we had handled it differently? Yes! But we didn't, and we will all have to live with that. What will it change if we go to the police now? It won't bring that boy back. Let's try to enjoy the rest of our time together. We never know what tomorrow may bring."

Robin and Shawna looked at each other. Robin went to her bag and grabbed a bottle of raspberry Bacardi and some red cups. We drank, cried, and sang.

A week later, I walked into our dorm room after class, and I found Shawna in the bath. The water was cherry red and a razor was floating on top. She had slit her wrist. On the floor outside of the tub, was a letter addressed to her parents and underneath were the words, "I am sorry."

I grabbed my face and then began to pace back and forth. I didn't know what to do, but I did know that I could not let the letter be found...so I took it and put it in my backpack. I went and grabbed Shawna's laptop and deleted her search history, so no one would be suspicious if they saw the article we read regarding the hit and run. I put the computer back on our old wooden table, and I started to scream. The RA ran into my room, and she saw Shawna. She pulled out her pink cell phone and called 911.

I called Robin, who made it to the dorm a few minutes after the police. They would not let her in the room, so I went out to her. I told Robin that I had found Shawna in the bathtub with her wrist slit. Robin said she had talked to Shawna earlier that day. Shawna told Robin about the argument that we had gotten into, and Robin was on her way before I called to pick Shawna up. Shawna told Robin that she was going to focus on school and try not to think about what happened over the summer.

The police asked both Robin and I a slew of questions. They asked me if I found a letter from Shawna. I told them no. The police said that most of the time, a person who died by suicide will leave a letter to say goodbye to loved ones and at least give some reason for taking their life. I, reluctantly, went to my dad's house later that night. I had nowhere else to go. I went into my room and pulled out the letter that Shawna had left for her parents. I read the letter over and over and over again, until it was etched into my brain.

*Dear Mom and Dad,*

*I am so sorry that I didn't listen to you, and that I went on that road trip. That was the biggest mistake of my life. I just wanted to prove that I was old enough to make good decisions on my own. The trip proved me wrong. I have attached a story about a young athlete who was killed by a hit and run accident three months ago.*

*I was the driver. I can no longer live with this guilt. The fact that I killed someone and left them there in a ditch on the side of the road is more than I can bear. I am sorry that I didn't come to you sooner and that I didn't call you after it happened. Maybe you would have been able to convince Morgan, Robin, and I to do the right thing.*

*I wanted to tell you so many times, but I knew that you would be very disappointed in me and with the overwhelming guilt that I already have, I knew it would be more than I could take. I am sorry... tell my Eli and Elizabeth that I love them.*

*Good bye,*

*Shawna*

Tears flowed down my cheeks and fell onto my teddy bear with the red bowtie that I was holding on to in a chokehold—the sadder I became, the tighter I held Teddy. I began to scream into the pillow.

I looked at the letter again. For a moment I thought about taking it to Shawna's parents. Then I looked around at my pink room with the flower border along the walls. I hated that room.

I looked over on the dresser and saw my neon-green lighter. I picked it up and lit the corner of the paper. It burned slowly, as I walked to my silver metal trash can. I tossed it in and watched the flames devour the letter.

I laid in the bed and began to stare at the walls. I had stared at those walls in my bedroom so many nights hoping and praying that the pain would end. I imagined the walls opening so that I could just run out, or that perhaps my father would sober up and come into the room and protect me from his disgusting brother. Neither ever happened. I can still smell the stale cigarette smoke on my uncle's clothes and his breath reeking of alcohol. Him whispering into my ear that if I made a noise, he would kill me and my dad. I wish I could burn those memories as easily as I burned away Shawna's letter. I could not ruin my future and potentially have to look at those four walls for the rest of my life, or even worse, spend the rest of my life in prison.

I called Robin several times that night and throughout the week. She didn't return my phone calls; the next time I saw her was at the funeral. She told me that it was our fault that Shawna was dead and that we should've let her confess if she wanted to. Robin blamed me, because it was my idea to take the road trip. That was the last time that I spoke to her. She eventually dropped out of college and moved away. My aunt told me that she started using drugs and was in and out of rehab.

# CHAPTER 13

Morgan looked up, and Mr. Calloway was looking at her as if she was a stranger. He cleared his throat and said, "That is quite a story. Morgan, to be honest, I don't know what to say. You were kids when this happened, but you have had plenty of time to come clean, and you did not. This does not look good. Your credibility will now come into question. I have to ask you something, and I need you to be completely honest with me. Were you in any way a part of the private investigator being murdered at your engagement party?"

Morgan looked him straight in his eyes and said, "No."

Mr. Calloway got up and walked across the room to her. To Morgan's surprise, he put his arms around her and told her that everything would be ok, and that, if he were her father, he would have protected her. Mr. Calloway promised her that he would be there for her, no matter what happened. Morgan began shivering; she buried her head into his chest and began to cry in his arms. The harder she cried, the closer he held her. He gently rubbed her head, reassuring her that everything would be ok.

Jean walked in and said, "Oh my, is everything ok?"

Mr. Calloway replied, "It will be. I will talk to you about it later, Jean. For right now, can you please get Morgan a glass of water?"

Mr. Calloway wiped Morgan's bangs from off her forehead and kissed it saying, "Morgan, I promise you. You are safe now."

Morgan so desperately needed to hear those words. She just wanted to be safe and feel stable—not living in fear of every man who crossed her path—hoping and praying that one day she would find a man who would erase all the hurt. She thought she found that in Andre, but just like every other man in her life, he betrayed her.

All of a sudden, she remembered...

Morgan threw her head back, grabbed her face, and she yelled, "Mr. Calloway! I remember! I know...I know that man that Andre murdered. He talked to me my first year in law school. He called our dorm room and asked for Shawna, saying that he was investigating the hit and run of that young man. He said he was hired by the family, and that Shawna left him a message, telling him that she had information about the incident. How could I forget? How could I totally block that out?"

Mr. Calloway said, "Morgan, I have worked with a lot of clients, and it's normal when you talk about a traumatic event recalling things that you may have suppressed. You have been deliberately trying to forget about what happened during that summer. Now that you are talking about these painful events, you are starting to remember things that you blocked out."

Jean walked back into the room with the glass of water. Morgan began to take slow sips, as she stared out the window, wondering what other horrific memories she had blocked out. Mr. Calloway told Jean that he and Morgan were heading down to the police station.

He looked at Morgan and said, "In order to show that you are not hiding anything at all, you must tell the detective everything, and that includes what happened when you were a teenager."

Morgan nodded her head, grabbed her coat, and they headed towards the door.

---

As they sat in the car waiting to go into the police station, Mr. Calloway said, "Morgan, do you know why I love swans so much?"

She said, "No."

He unfastened his seat belt and turned towards Morgan. He said, "Swans can represent so many things, but one of their most intriguing qualities is their loyalty. They mate for life. They are always together. They also represent strength. The black swan, for example, is very unique; there are so many myths and stories about it. There is something called "The Black Swan Theory" that, in essence, describes an event that comes as a surprise, and results in a major impact to the environment or a person's personal life. It is rationalized after the fact, with the benefit of hindsight. You are like that black swan. You were involved in something that changed the course of your life, and looking back now, you wish you handled it differently. It's too late to change the past, but you can make this right."

# CHAPTER 14

The room that Officer Paddington sat Morgan and Mr. Calloway in was different from the first room that Morgan had an interview in. This room seemed less friendly—it was very uncomfortable and that is exactly what Detective McKnight wanted. It had cement walls and there were only four chairs in the room. The temperature was extremely cold and it had no windows. Sticking out of one of the corners, was a camera pointed directly at the seat that Officer Paddington sat Morgan in. Morgan's heart began to race, and her knees were bouncing uncontrollably.

Mr. Calloway gently put his hand on her knee and said, "Morgan, I know that this is very unnerving, and that you are scared. Just remember to be honest, and the most important thing, is that you do not say a word unless I give you the ok."

Morgan nodded, reminiscing on all the times that she had said the same thing to her clients; and the thought of never being able to repeat that line again was nauseating. She understood the seriousness of the situation that she was in. It could affect her future—after this interview, she could be disbarred...or even worse, imprisoned. She started to snap the band on her wrist. This was such a nightmare.

Detective McKnight entered the room. In one hand, he had a file full of papers, and in the other hand, he had a coffee...he apologized for keeping them waiting.

Mr. Calloway cleared his throat and said, "Ok, Detective, there are some things that are sensitive that I feel you need to know, and the information is pertinent to the conversation that you had with Robin Harris. We are not sure, however, if it is connected in any way to the murder at the engagement party. We need your word that what we tell you will be off the record. It is very delicate, and many lives can be destroyed if the information is not released in the right way. I would look at this as a huge favor to me. I am more than Morgan's attorney; she is like a daughter to me."

Detective McKnight shook his head in agreement.

"Whatever you say, Ms. Waters, will be off the record...for now. However, if I feel that it becomes an integral part of my investigation, I will have to make District Attorney Hughes aware of it."

Mr. Calloway said, "Go ahead, Morgan, tell Detective McKnight what you know about the man that Andre murdered."

Morgan took a deep breath and began to rub her hands together. They were very dry and cracked from the cold. She opened her purse and grabbed a bottle of Oak & Sweet Almond Hemp lotion and began to rub it into her hands.

She said, "Detective McKnight, I just recently realized that I do know the man that Andre murdered. I guess I had blocked him out of my mind, because he is from a past that I have worked really hard to forget. He questioned me my freshman year in college about a hit and run accident that happened in Tennessee."

Detective McKnight said, "Why did he question you about something like that?"

Morgan looked at Mr. Calloway; he nodded his head for her to answer the question.

Morgan rubbed her hands back in forth over her jeans, and then ran them through her hair. She took a deep breath and said, "The private investigator said that he had received a phone call from my friend Shawna Smith; she told him that she had some information regarding the hit and run. I told him that she had passed away, and that I could not help him. He asked If I had any knowledge of the incident, and I told him no."

Detective McKnight said, "And *did* you know anything about the hit and run?"

Mr. Calloway leaned on the table and said, "This is part of the information that we need to stay off the record. At least until we figure out our next move."

Detective McKnight shook his head again.

Morgan said, "Yes...it was my car that hit the teenager; I was a passenger. Shawna was the one that hit him while we were driving down a dark road. We got out of the car and moved his body to a ditch, and then we called the police. We tried to pretend like it didn't happen, but it was too much for Shawna to deal with, so she killed herself, and Robin blames me for her death."

Detective McKnight began to loosen his black-and-gray, silk necktie and said,

"I think we can all use a break. Let's continue the interview in about 20 minutes."

Morgan asked Detective McKnight if they had a vending machine, and he pointed down the hall. Mr. Calloway said that he was going to Starbucks to grab a coffee. Morgan asked him to get her a caramel brûlée; it's a seasonal drink, and she treated herself to one at least once a week.

Morgan saw Detective McKnight in the hallway on the phone as she headed back to the interview room with her yellow bag of peanut M&Ms. He looked like he in a very intense conversation. She tried to act like she couldn't hear, but his voice became louder and louder. He was talking to someone name Shelia, telling her that she needed to make sure that she was home this time when he came by to pick up his sons. He looked and saw that Morgan was listening.

Detective McKnight said, "Mr. Calloway is not back yet; you can have a seat in the room, and I'll be in there momentarily."

A few minutes later, Detective McKnight walked into the room.

Morgan said, "Detective McKnight, I hope that I am not sounding intrusive, but I heard the conversation you had on the phone when I was walking by. I am assuming you were talking with your wife regarding your kids. I am so sorry about what you are going through. You do know that she cannot legally keep you from your kids. If she is not showing up to scheduled parenting times you can petition the court to set up the times, and there would be a judge's order in place compelling her to meet you at the agreed-upon time. Just some free advice."

He smiled and said, "Thank you, but Shelia is having a rough time right now. It wasn't easy being married to me, and I haven't always been the best husband. I know that she will realize that her behavior is not benefiting the kids and will come around. She may not like me much right now, but she loves our kids, and she will do what is in the best interest of them."

Morgan exclaimed, "I hope that she comes to that realization quickly. You know your kids need you. They need both parents. I know how hard it is being a child and wanting both parents around. Trust me, you don't want your children to go through that."

Mr. Calloway walked in the room carrying two venti drinks from Starbucks and said, "I hope you haven't been questioning my client without me, young man."

Detective McKnight stood up as Mr. Calloway walked by and said, "I can guarantee you, I was not. Morgan was just giving me some free legal advice."

Mr. Calloway chuckled and said, "Morgan, I know I taught you better than that—giving away billable advice."

They all laughed. Morgan thanked Mr. Calloway for her drink.

Mr. Calloway grabbed her hand and said, "Morgan, you are doing the right thing; I am so proud of you."

She smiled and exhaled, and then took another sip of her coffee.

This was something Morgan had never experienced before; having someone in her corner with no strings attached. Mr. Calloway is like the father that she always dreamed of. One that was the complete opposite of her loser of a father.

Detective McKnight asked Morgan a few more questions and said, "I think I have enough information for now. Please do not leave town, Ms. Waters. I will keep the information about the hit and run quiet for now."

Morgan's face frowned, "Don't leave town? Am I a suspect?"

"You are not a suspect, but a very important witness...and I would like you to stay close in case anything comes up, and we need to talk to you."

Morgan hissed, "Fine!"

She said fine, but she had a flight going out to Ohio in a couple of days to see Robin, and she was not going to cancel. She knew that Detective McKnight could ask, but that didn't mean she had to comply unless a judge ordered her not to leave town. Still, she decided not to mention her trip to Detective McKnight or to Mr. Calloway, to be safe.

# CHAPTER 15

Detective McKnight had a funny feeling in his stomach. He usually felt that way when something didn't sit right with him. He didn't know if he was disturbed about what Ms. Waters told him, if it was because of the suspicious blue van that was driving by her house earlier, or if it was because he was keeping important information from District Attorney Hughes...whatever the reason, he felt unsettled.

He sat down in his chair at home and started reading over his notes. He knew there had to be a connection between the hit and run, Andre Williams, and the private investigator. For the life of him, he could not figure it out. He read over everything again and then decided it may be beneficial for him to take a trip to Tennessee; maybe the missing piece could be found there.

He called his Captain to share his thoughts and concerns, and she agreed that it would be a good idea for Sean to fly out to Tennessee. She told him that before he went out there, he needed to reach out to the local law enforcement office. The Captain knew that Sean could be presumptuous, and she didn't want him going to Tennessee stepping on any toes.

CHAPTER 15

As soon as he hung up with the Captain, he called the police department in the small town in Tennessee, and he talked to Sheriff Walker. This was the second time they had spoken; the first time, was when Detective McKnight asked Sheriff Walker if he would notify the family of private investigator, Johnathan Grey's, death.

After getting off the phone with Sheriff Walker, Detective McKnight decided to try to get some sleep. He tossed and turned; he put the pillow over his head and then took it off and hugged it. Nothing he tried could help him sleep, so he decided he would go for a drive.

This had become a custom when a case stumped him. It helped to clear his mind, driving and breathing in the fresh air. It always drove Shelia crazy; she couldn't understand why he would leave at one or two o'clock in the morning to go on a drive.

He decided to drive by Ms. Waters' house. As he was turning onto her block, he noticed the blue van that they had issued a BOLO on. He picked up the CB radio in his car and called it in, asking for back up at Ms. Waters' house. His heart began to race as he approached the vehicle. He pushed the gas all the way to the ground and pulled up next to the car that was sitting on the side street.

He decided not to wait for back up, because if it was Andre Williams, Detective McKnight did not want him to flee the scene. He pulled his gun out of the holster and began to approach the vehicle. He pressed his body up against the driver's side of the car and walked towards the door. He pulled the door open and stuck his gun inside; he looked in the back seat of the van and then popped the trunk—the van was completely empty.

Detective McKnight began to run to Morgan's house. His legs were sore from his run the day before, but he could not let the pain slow him down. He ran up her driveway and knocked on the window of Ms. Waters' protection detail; the officer was on the phone. Detective McKnight told him to back him up: as they approached the door, they heard a piercing scream. Detective McKnight jiggled the knob to see if it was open. The door was locked, so he moved back, pulled his leg as far back as he could, and kicked the door in. They heard a loud commotion from upstairs. Usually, they would clear the room they were in, but there was no time. Detective McKnight and the officer ran upstairs to see Andre Williams on top of Morgan Waters...choking her.

Detective McKnight yelled, "Freeze! It's the police!"

Andre looked up. His eyes were blood-shot red, and he reeked of alcohol. Andre let go of Morgan's neck and shoved her towards Detective McKnight. He ran toward the open window, looked back and stepped on the window sill, and jumped. Detective McKnight ran behind him and jumped out of the window.

Detective McKnight landed on the snow-covered bush under the window. He rolled off of the bush onto the ground, and he could see Andre running away. He knew that he had to catch Andre; he could not let him get away. He put his hand on the ground and pushed himself up.

Detective McKnight looked at the ground and started in the direction of the fresh shoeprints in the snow. The one thing that he had in his favor, was that he was a track-and-field star in high school, and he still held the record at the department for being the fastest sprinter.

He saw Andre and yelled, "Stop! Police!" Detective McKnight was far ahead of his backup. His heart was racing, and he felt a little pain in his knee from jumping out of the window, but he didn't let that slow him down. Andre ran to the van, fumbling with the keys to open it, but his hands were sweaty and shaky, and he dropped them on the ground. As he bent down to pick up the keys, Detective McKnight lunged towards him and knocked him on the ground.

Andre took his hands and tried to grab Detective McKnight to get him off of him. The more he wiggled and punched, the tighter

Detective McKnight's grip became. Desperate, Andre opened his mouth and bit Detective McKnight's hand as hard as he could.

Detective McKnight screamed out and loosened his grip. Andre lunged forward, only to be met by McKnight's foot. He lost his balance and fell back to the ground.

Detective McKnight yelled, "Stop resisting!!"

His backup arrived and yelled, "Taser!"

The officer aimed the taser at Andre and jolted him with 50,000 volts of electricity. Andre began shaking, his arms were flailing, and his legs jumped with every jolt. After a few minutes, Detective McKnight and the officer were able to pull Andre's hands behind his back and put cuffs on him. They each grabbed an arm and pulled him to his feet. Detective McKnight read him his rights before sticking him in the backseat of the cruiser.

Although exhausted from the pursuit, Detective McKnight ran back up to Morgan's house. He was not sure of her condition, and he prayed all the way back to her front door that she was ok. He had promised her before that they would catch Andre, and nothing would happen to her. When he approached the house, he saw blue and red lights flashing from the police cars and the ambulance.

EMTs were pulling a stretcher out of the house with Morgan lying on it.

Detective McKnight ran to her and grabbed her hand saying, "We got him! Andre is in police custody. He will never hurt you or anyone else again."

Morgan whispered, "Thank you! Can you please ride with me? I am afraid, and I don't want to be alone."

The EMTs lifted her into the ambulance and one of them put their hand out to help Detective McKnight in.

The female EMT, who had her blond hair pulled up in a ponytail said, "Detective, you don't look well. Your eyes are dilated, and you look flushed...I think we should take your vitals."

Detective McKnight sat back as she pulled out a blood pressure cuff and strapped it on his arm.

"Oh, no, Detective, your hand is punctured, and you are bleeding! Did the suspect bite you?"

Detective McKnight looking down at his hand replied, "Yes, he did."

"We need to clean that up, and we should have the doctor look at it. The bite is pretty deep."

Detective McKnight said, "My main concern right now is Ms. Waters. We can worry about my hand later."

Detective McKnight looked over at Morgan and said, "Morgan, are you ok? I am so sorry that he was able to get to you. Do you know how he got into your house?"

Morgan responded, "When I came home, he was waiting for me in my room. I don't know how he got in. I'm so scared that he is not going to stop until he kills me."

Morgan sat up on the stretcher, pulled her knees to her chest, and buried her head. She began to cry uncontrollably, and the EMT gave her some meds to calm her down.

Detective McKnight called Mr. Calloway to tell him what happened.

Mr. Calloway yelled, "How could you all let this happen? Where was her police escort? This is unacceptable. Andre never should have been able to get anywhere near her. I will meet you at the hospital."

While in the ambulance, Detective McKnight also called his captain to let her know what happened, and that Andre Williams was in custody. His captain said that she would call DA Hughes and bring him up to date.

Sean hated hospitals; they brought up so many bad memories. The worst being the day that he held his mother's hand as she took her last breath. He would never forget the sound of air exiting her lungs, and her frail body going motionless. The numbness he felt that day returned every time he stepped foot into the hospital. As he walked down the hall, he wondered how many families would be mourning their loved ones tonight.

Detective McKnight saw Mr. and Mrs. Calloway rushing around the corner. He flagged them down and gave them details about what happened; then the Calloways went into Morgan's room. Detective McKnight left and headed toward the police station, hoping to get some answers from Andre Williams.

# CHAPTER 16

When he entered the station, he asked the officers where they had taken Mr. Williams; the officers said that he had asked for his attorney, and that they had put him in holding. Detective McKnight was upset with himself. He knew that he should have driven Andre to the police station, instead of going to the hospital, but he couldn't leave Ms. Waters alone in the state that she was in.

Mr. Calloway called Sean and said that when the hospital released Morgan, he was going to take her back to his house with him and Jean. Detective McKnight told him that he thought that would be a good idea.

The night was very stressful, but Detective McKnight was happy that they finally had Andre in custody and that Ms. Waters was ok. He decided to call it a night. He wanted to go home and soak in Epsom salt; every inch of his body was sore, and he needed to try and get a couple of hours of sleep before Andre's arraignment in the morning.

Frank Hughes called Detective McKnight and asked for all the evidence in the case, and said he had a few questions before the arraignment. He wanted to know if the evidence could support the charges of first-degree murder and attempted murder. Detective McKnight said they had him dead to rights on attempted murder, but he was still trying to find out the motive for the murder of private investigator, Johnathan Grey. Did he intend to kill the PI, or was it in the heat of the moment? The intent was necessary for the first-degree murder charge. DA Hughes was not happy, but he was going to arraign Andre on the lesser charge, and when they gathered more evidence, he would add additional charges.

Detective McKnight went to the arraignment. He was happy to see Andre in the orange jailhouse suit and cuffs. He had a smirk on his face, like he didn't care that he was caught. Detective McKnight wanted to smack that smirk off.

He was hoping that his trip to Tennessee would give more insight into PI Grey and what his connection was with Andre, if there was any.

The judge remanded Andre without bail. Detective McKnight called Mr. Calloway, so he could tell Morgan the good news.

Detective McKnight decided to head home to get ready for his trip. He no longer looked forward to going; it saddened him just thinking about entering the house with his boys not being there.

He was shaken back to reality by the loud ring coming across the speaker in his car. It was DA Frank Hughes.

"Hi, Frank."

Frank replied, "Andre's attorney called my office. He wants to make a plea. He said that he has evidence implicating Morgan Waters. Can you believe that!! Morgan has been playing the victim all this time and may very well have been involved in the murder from the beginning. Do you know that cases like these are what makes careers? Look, Sean, I would like you to tag along when I go to the jail to talk to Andre Williams and his Attorney."

Detective McKnight would be perfectly fine with never having to enter the jail. It had a musty smell that gets stuck in your nose. As he walked to the interview room, he saw many lifeless faces: some who deserved to be in jail, and others he wasn't sure should be there. He walked past the cafeteria and heard arguing and cussing. He saw a boy no older than 17 sitting in a corner, looking down, trying not to give any of the other inmates a reason to come and bother him.

That could've been Detective McKnight, if he didn't have the strong, loving grandmother that he had. He didn't have many good role models growing up. He didn't remember his dad—he walked out on his mom when he was a baby—and growing up, his mom dated a loser, so his life was not very stable until his mother died, and he moved in with his grandmother.

As Detective McKnight was walking up the hall, he saw Frank standing by the attorney's room. Frank was always dressed like a million bucks. He stood about 6'3 and was 200 pounds of pure muscle. He had a nicely manicured mustache and beard, and was wearing a tailored blue suit with brown Oxfords, that matched his brown belt. He was on his phone when McKnight walked up.

Frank said, "Hello, Sean. Mr. Williams is talking to his lawyer; as soon as they are done, we can go in."

A few minutes later, the door to the interview room opened; and they were greeted by a chubby, short man, with untrusting eyes. They saw Andre Williams, and they went and sat at the opposite side of the table.

Frank said, "Okay, you asked for this meeting...what do you have for me?"

The attorney replied, "My client wants a deal. He will tell you what he knows about the murder, and everyone involved, if you would promise to give him a reduced sentence and let him serve his time concurrently. He also wants to be close to his family in Tennessee, so that they can visit."

When the attorney said that Andre had family from Tennessee as well, it made Detective McKnight even more anxious to get down there to see what he could find out.

Detective McKnight said, "I thought you had no family, Mr. Williams...at least, isn't that what you told Ms. Waters?"

Andre peered through Detective McKnight with his cold, dark eyes and said, "Yes, I did. I told Morgan a lot of things."

Detective McKnight replied, "Mr. Williams, you are a liar and a con artist...how can you expect us to believe anything that you say?"

Andre smiled and said, "Detective, you don't have to believe me; I didn't invite you here. I'm here to talk to the man who can agree to the plea deal." Andre turned his body towards his attorney and said, "I will only talk to the District Attorney."

District Attorney Hughes said, "Ok, I'm listening. What do you have that would warrant me agreeing to the plea?"

Detective McKnight sighed heavily, then rolled his eyes and said, "I can't believe that we are entertaining this narcissist."

Frank looked at him and said, "Detective McKnight, let's see what he has to say."

Andre began, "I will admit that I did stab that private investigator, but I did it because Morgan asked me to. I would do anything that Morgan asked me to do. Have you ever looked at her beautiful face and her perfect body? She had a way of asking me to do something, and I always did it no questions asked. She was going to be my wife; it was my job to protect her, and that's what I did. Any real man would."

Frank interrupted, "You are telling me that Morgan Waters, your fiancée, who you strangled and left for dead at Mr. Calloway's home, asked you to kill Private Investigator Grey?"

Andrew replied, "That was all part of her plan, but she double-crossed me and told the police that I did it. That's why, I went back to finish the job. I couldn't believe that she betrayed me."

Detective McKnight said, "Ok, ok, ok...Mr. Williams, you want us to believe that this highly respected attorney, who you tried to kill twice, asked you to murder a man?"

Andre began to move his neck from side to side and said, "All I know is what Morgan told me. She said that he was someone from her past that was coming to ruin her. That if the information that he had got out, everything she had worked for would be gone. The life that she was building for us would be ruined. I have to admit, I loved the life that Morgan's job provided us, and I didn't want to lose that either, but I had no reason to kill the man. She told me that we had to get rid of him, so I did."

Detective McKnight turned away and walked to the window. He didn't want the look of shock on his face to be noticed by anyone in the room. He began to wonder, could Andre be telling the truth? It is odd that Morgan said she had never seen the PI before, but then, when she came to her interview with Mr. Calloway, she suddenly remembered him. Did she pull the wool over my eyes?

DA Hughes said, "Do you have any evidence to back up your story?"

Andre slammed his elbows on the table, clenched his fists, and a diabolical smile spread across his face...then he said, "The man's dead body is all the evidence you need."

He looked at his attorney who said, "This interview is over. Let us know if you decide to take the deal. If I were you Frank, I would really consider that, since this is an election year. No one likes a cover up; it can destroy careers."

District Attorney Hughes said, "Is that a threat? And it is District Attorney Hughes to you."

The attorney looked at him with a half grin and said, "No, not a threat, Frank...I mean, DA Hughes; it's just professional courtesy. I would hate to see a fellow attorney throw his career away over a bad decision."

Frank grabbed his briefcase and exited the room like Usain Bolt...and McKnight followed.

"Frank, slow down." Detective McKnight said.

Frank replied, "Who does that secondhand attorney think he is? How dare he threatens me or imply that I can't do my job. He is right though; we have to look into Morgan Waters. If it looks like I am showing favoritism to her because she is a successful attorney who works for Calloway and Associates, it wouldn't go well for me during the election. I want her brought in for questioning; and this time, not in an interview room, but into interrogation."

Detective McKnight didn't put up much of a fight. He was still thinking about the interview that he had with Robin Harris. She said some of the same things that Andre said about Ms. Waters. A little too similar for his liking.

Detective McKnight walked to his car; the cold brisk wind hit his face. Then, he felt an all too familiar feeling: wet, cold, sprinkles on his face—it was snowing. He turned his stroll into a jog. Then he sat in the car as it warmed up, watching each snowflake melt as soon as they hit his car windows.

He called Mr. Calloway to see if Morgan was released from the hospital. Mr. Calloway said she had been released earlier and was at his house now, but was insisting on going home and getting her life back to normal now that Andre was behind bars...so he would be dropping her off soon.

Detective McKnight told him that they needed come back to the station soon to answer some more questions. He let Mr. Calloway know that his call was just a courtesy. Morgan was not under arrest, but she had been implicated in the murder.

He replied, "Unfortunately, my client is unable to come to the station and answer any questions right now. She is recovering from an attack, and she is not in any condition to talk to the police."

Detective McKnight replied, "I will be out of town for a couple of days following a lead, but we would need to talk as soon as I get back."

Mr. Calloway reluctantly agreed.

Detective McKnight began to go over the evidence again, and when he looked up at the clock, a couple of hours had gone by.

As he was leaving the station, his Captain stopped him in the hall. She asked him to come to her office. They had been friends for years—she was the one who persuaded Sean to join the Providence police department after he left the academy.

When he entered her office, she let out a heavy sigh and said, "I just got off the phone with DA Hughes. He is not happy with you. He said that you held back a statement from a witness that could implicate Ms. Waters in the crime."

Detective McKnight said, "If you are talking about Robin Harris, I didn't feel that she was credible. I could punch a million holes all through her story."

"Well, District Attorney Hughes disagrees; he feels that along with Andre Williams' statement, it is enough to bring Ms. Waters in."

"I disagree, Cap. We don't have any hard evidence connecting Ms. Waters. We just have the word of a confessed murderer."

"This is out of my hands, Sean. DA Hughes already issued a warrant for her arrest. I sent two officers out to her home."

# CHAPTER 17

Morgan hopped out of bed. It sounded like someone was trying to break down her front door. Her heart began to pound. She knew that Andre was arrested, but she couldn't shake the feeling that it was him trying to come and finish her off. She went over and peeked out of the window, and saw two police cars in her driveway.

She grabbed her phone off the nightstand and called Detective McKnight.

"Hello, this is Detective McKnight."

"Detective McKnight, this is Morgan. There are police banging on my front door. Did you know about this?"

"I am on my way to your house now. I just found out that DA Hughes issued a warrant for your arrest. Listen to me, do not open the door. I am on my way...call Mr. Calloway."

Morgan hung up and called Mr. Calloway. He said that he was going to call the DA to see what was going on. She went to her closet and grabbed a pair of blue jeans and a red sweater. Then, she went into the bathroom, brushed her teeth, and put her hair in a ponytail. She began to snap her pink band over and over again, as she paced the floor. When she looked down, she had a welt from where the band had snapped. She began to rub her wrist and looked out the window again, hoping that the police cars would be gone.

Her phone buzzed, and she looked down; it was her doorbell. She saw Detective McKnight standing at the door, so she ran down the stairs and opened it.

He said, "I am going to take you to the police station. Mr. Calloway will meet us there. I know the officers, and they agreed to let me take you in."

Morgan began to pray—something she hadn't done since her mother died. Her phone rang again; it was Mr. Calloway calling her back; he told Morgan that he would be at the jail, and that she must not to say anything else until he was present. She walked out the front door, escorted by Detective McKnight.

Morgan held her head down to ensure that she did not make eye contact with any of her neighbors. She really only knew a few of them, because she was always working, so even though she had been there for years, she never had the time to attend any neighborhood functions. She only knew the names of two families.

One was the Cowlings; they had a daughter and two sons. She would pay the boys sometimes to do little jobs in her yard. Then there was Ms. Blake; she was in her 60's and was 5'2 and fierce. She was also a professor of African American studies at one of the local colleges. Ms. Blake was the first neighbor that Morgan met; she is a very nice woman, and a widow. When Morgan first moved into her home, Ms. Blake brought her a zucchini bread— she told Morgan that she loved to bake, and that she used to make them for her late husband. She talked about how much he loved to have a piece in the morning, warmed up with a little butter to go along with his coffee. She would occasionally go over to visit Morgan, and they would talk about life and the plight of women of color; and how far they had come, but how far they still had to go.

Morgan wondered what they were thinking of her now. Seeing

police cars at her house for the second time in a week; knowing that her fiancé was charged with murder and tried to kill her. She could only imagine the headlines: *Attorney from the Prestigious Law Firm, Calloway and Associates Arrested for Conspiracy to Murder.* She sat quiet in the backseat as Detective McKnight drove to the station.

Detective McKnight looked in his rear-view mirror, and he saw Morgan's tear-stained face. He said, "Ms. Waters, is there anything you want to tell me? I can help you, if you are honest with me."

She whispered, "Detective, you know that you should not be asking me any questions without my attorney present."

The rest of the car ride was silent. Detective McKnight began to wonder if he put his career on the line trying to protect the reputation of a murderer. He knew that he had been off his game since the beginning of the case. He had so much on his mind with everything going on in his personal life, and it made him wonder if he missed something. Did he allow Ms. Waters' charm to influence his decisions? Was he so blinded by her beauty and intelligence that it tricked him into believing that she could not be capable of being involved in a murder?

Detective McKnight pulled up to the police station, got out of the car, and opened the back door for Morgan. She put her head down again, as they hurried into the station. Detective McKnight walked beside Morgan, trying to protect her the best he could from the cameras. Someone had leaked the story to the news, and they were all outside of the station awaiting her arrival. Detective McKnight was sure it was District Attorney Hughes. He loved to be in front of the cameras, and with this being an election year, this case could win or lose it for him.

Morgan was so grateful that Detective McKnight had not put handcuffs on her. She would not have been able to bear the humiliation. As they walked into the station, standing at the front desk, were Officer Paddington and District Attorney Hughes. DA Hughes looked like the cat who ate the canary. He was enjoying it all a little too much, and it annoyed Detective McKnight. They walked right passed the DA without saying anything, and Detective McKnight took Morgan down to central booking.

While waiting to see Morgan, Mr. Calloway walked up to Mr. Hughes and said, "You just couldn't help yourself, could you, young man? You are so concerned with being in the press from this case and being reelected, that you are not even looking for the truth. Let me tell you something, son. I have a lot, and I mean a lot of powerful friends in this city, and I am going to use every single one of them to make sure that Morgan is treated fairly...and who knows? After this, I may run for DA." He walked away not giving DA Hughes a chance to respond.

District Attorney Hughes called Detective McKnight and said, "I need to see you in your office, now."

Detective McKnight told him that after Morgan was processed, he would be back up to his office.

After 30 minutes, Detective McKnight was walking back to his office, and saw District Attorney Hughes pacing the halls.

Detective McKnight walked into his office, and District Attorney Hughes walked in behind him, slammed the door and said, "Did you think I would not find out about the interview with you and Ms. Harris? I could have your job for this! I see how you look at Ms. Waters. Can I trust you to be unbiased investigating this case, or should I ask your Captain to assign it to another detective?"

"Are you kidding me! You are doing all of this for reelection. You don't even care about the truth Frank. I told you I am still investigating and that I didn't, and still don't find Ms. Harris or Mr. Williams reliable witnesses. Tell me Frank, what experience do have with the investigating side of a case? You know what? Take the little evidence that you have and pursue it. I can guarantee you will not have the outcome that you want. Another thing, Frank, don't ever threaten me again. I promise you that won't go the way you would like it to, either. Get out of my office I have work to do."

# CHAPTER 18

"Thank you, Judge!" Mr. Calloway said. He walked over to District Attorney Hughes and said, "Young man, I am just getting started."

Mrs. Calloway was in the courtroom to support Morgan. She made it perfectly clear to Mr. Calloway that she was very disappointed in Morgan, and she didn't know if she would ever look at her the same, but she loved her and would support her, no matter what.

The judge allowed Morgan to leave on her own recognizance, under the condition that she stayed with the Calloways in their home, and she could not leave the state. District Attorney Hughes was furious that the judge released Morgan. He had asked that she be remanded to jail.

The judge is an old golfing buddy of Mr. Calloway, and they had been friends for over 30 years. Jean and the judge's wife were best friends, and the Calloways spent countless hours with the judge when his dear wife died. There really weren't many judges, businessmen, or politicians who the Calloways did not know.

"Morgan, please sit down...you have been pacing since we've gotten here. We need to come up with a strategy for your defense." Mr. Calloway said.

"I'm trying to remain calm, but I just can't believe that I am in this position. I'm the victim! Andre killed Private Investigator Grey, then he tried to kill me. All he had to do was make the accusation that I had something to do with it, and without any other proof, that DA has me arrested."

"Well, Morgan, it is an election year. I did my homework on District Attorney Hughes, and he is an ambitious young fellow; but I think that he is reasonable and fair. If we can convince him of your innocence, I am sure that he will drop these outrageous charges. How would you feel about taking a polygraph?"

"What...don't you believe me?"

"Of course, I believe you dear, but it would give us some leverage. The District Attorney would have to rethink his whole position. Who is he going to believe? A polygraph, or a man who would say anything to have his sentence reduced?"

"Sure, I will do it."

Mr. Calloway went over to his rolodex and began flipping through it. "I am going to call one of my friends; he has a very good reputation doing polygraphs...he retired from the FBI and opened his business. I'll see when he can administer the test."

Mr. Calloway walked away to make the call, and Morgan began to flick the pink band on her arm again. She thought, *What if I fail the polygraph? What then?* She knew innocent people who went to jail, and the polygraph was essential to the reason they were convicted.

Morgan was confident that she would pass. She knew that she would have to remain calm and try her best to answer the questions honestly. She began to wonder, if during the administering of the test, the examiner would ask her anything that she would have to lie about from her past. She knew that she had things that she never wanted to come out.

Jean came into the room with a cup of tea. "Here you are, Morgan. Hopefully, this will help you calm down, and you can get some rest."

Smiling, she replied, "Thank you, Jean." Morgan grabbed Jean's hand as she turned to walk away and said, "Jean, I know Mr. Calloway told you what happened when I was a teenager. I hope you don't look at me differently. I was a kid, who made a bad decision—I had no one who I could go to for advice...I was so alone as a teenager. My mother was the one person who I could talk to about anything, and she was gone. I was so lost. You have to believe me, Jean...I was so lost."

Jean said, "Honey, I am not here to judge you. We have all done things that we wish we could change. If I am being honest, when Henry first told me about what you had done when you were a teenager, I was very disappointed. I'm so sorry, Morgan, that you had no one to go to, but you have me and Henry now; and we are here for you, no matter what."

Jean reached out and put her arms around Morgan. Morgan laid her head on Jean's shoulder and enjoyed every second of her embrace.

Mr. Calloway walked into the room and said, "Morgan, your polygraph is set up for tomorrow at 10:00 a.m. Now, you have had a long couple of days, and you look exhausted. You need to be well rested for the test tomorrow...why don't you go on upstairs and lie down and get yourself some rest."

---

Morgan woke up to Jean knocking on her door.

Jean said, "Rise and shine. You have a long day ahead of you."

Morgan looked up, and Jean had a silver tray in her hand. On it, was a vegan breakfast casserole, toast, orange juice, and coffee.

Morgan was not hungry, because she was so nervous about the test, but to be polite, she took the tray and thanked Jean.

An hour later, Mr. Calloway knocked at the door and said, "Morgan, the bus leaves in 10 minutes...he laughed and walked away."

The drive to the test was long. Mr. Calloway played Al Green and occasionally sang along with him. He had a beautiful voice, and used to sing at some of the local joints when he was a teenager. In fact, that is where he met Jean. She and her sisters would go to the clubs to listen to the performers. Once Jean heard Henry sing, she made sure that she was there every time he performed. One night, Henry walked over to her, and they started to talk; from that day on, they were inseparable.

Mr. Calloway let Morgan out at the front door and went to park his black Benz. Morgan was too nervous to go into the office alone, so she waited for him to park. They walked in together; the sign on the front door said Paul's Poly's. They were met by a young woman, who told them that Mr. Granger would be right with them.

Paul Granger stepped out of his office and said, "Hello, Henry, good to see you...and you must be Morgan Waters."

He was a tall slender man, with a baby face. He had on a brown suit, with a yellow-and-brown striped tie on. Morgan couldn't believe he was the same age as Mr. Calloway. He walked with a limp, and Morgan began to wonder if that was an injury from his days in the FBI.

"Morgan, would you like some water?" Paul asked.

"Yes, that would be nice."

He yelled out to his secretary to bring in a bottle of water.

"Morgan, I will you have you sit here."

Morgan looked at the chair there was a metal plate sitting on it and on the floor where she would need to place her feet. There were other wires to be connected to her, but she wasn't sure where he thought he would be putting them.

Mr. Granger said, "Just a few things before we get started. I need to check your shoes. You know that some people have tried to put a tack in their shoe to step on when answering questions to increase their blood pressure or pulse rate and alter the results. But a good tester knows that it is other cues that you consider as well, when reading the results. Some people are professional liars, not because they are bad people, but because of their jobs...they have gotten used to being deceitful to make a sale. I pride myself over the fact that I have interviewed some of the most devious and evil people you could imagine, and for the most part, I was able to tell whether they were being deceitful or not."

When Paul was in the FBI, he was a specialist for The National Center for the Analysis of Violent Crime. He helped law enforcement agencies who were investigating unusual or repetitive violent crimes. Paul sat on interviews with some of the world's most dangerous criminals.

Morgan replied, "Well, that is good to know; but I promise I don't have any tacks touching these well-manicured feet."

"I am going to hook a few sensors on you, and then I will start asking you some questions. How does that sound?"

"I just want this over with, so I can prove my innocence and clear my name."

"I will start with some baseline questions, and then we will get into the reason you are here. I want you to try to relax and be completely honest with me. I have been doing this for many years. Right now, you are the only one who knows the truth, but after I complete the test we both will know."

Morgan opened the bottle of water and took a sip. She said, "I am ready when you are."

"What is your name?"

"Morgan Waters."

"Are the lights off?"

"No."

"Are you sitting?"

"Yes."

"Are you an attorney?"

"Yes."

"Have you ever stolen anything in your life?"

"Yes."

These questions went on for a couple of hours. Paul gave Morgan a break. She greatly appreciated it. All the questions had given her a headache, and she needed a bathroom break. Morgan walked slowly back into the interview room.

Paul said, "Just a few more questions, and we will be done with this portion of the test. I will then go analyze your answers and will have the results."

"Have you ever betrayed anyone who trusted you?"

"No."

"Have you ever murdered anyone?"

"No."

"Have you ever conspired to have anyone murdered?"

"No."

"Ok, Morgan, we are done. Would you like Henry to come back here with you while you wait for the results?"

"Yes, please."

Paul stepped out of the room to grab Mr. Calloway. Morgan breathed with a sigh of relief, happy that the polygraph was over.

It usually would take Paul at least 24 hours to get the results and report back to his clients, but he was doing a favor for Mr. Calloway. He told them that he would give them his preliminary findings, but they would have to wait for the official report.

Mr. Calloway walked into the room. He saw the worry that was all over Morgan's face, and once again assured her that she was doing the right thing. He then told her that he was on the phone with the attorney from the White case that they had been working on. The attorney told Mr. Calloway that his client was ready to settle the case. This made Morgan happy.

Mrs. White lost her son to cancer. She came to Calloway and Associates because she was sure that he caught cancer from exposure to dangerous chemicals on his job. Mrs. White had gathered a group of people who lost loved ones to the same type of cancer, who worked for the same company, and Calloway and Associates were representing them in a class-action lawsuit.

Mr. Calloway and Morgan were looking over the proposed settlement that the attorney had emailed to Mr. Calloway, and Paul walked back into the room.

He sat down and said, "Like I said before, this is just a preliminary finding. Morgan, I found no deceit in your answers, so my professional opinion is that you are telling the truth. After I do a thorough review of everything, I will have my secretary type up the report and email it to you. It was really nice meeting you, Morgan, and I hope that this will help clear your name."

Morgan let out a sigh of relief and said, "Thank you, so do I."

Mr. Calloway said, "Paul, it is always a pleasure. Let's get together soon for that dinner you owe me. You know from when you lost..."

Paul interrupted, "No need to bring up old news, Henry, we will get together for that meal soon." Henry started his loud infectious laugh, and Paul joined in.

"I'm going to hold you to that, Paul. I'll talk to you soon."

"Henry, please send Jean my love."

"Will do, my friend."

As soon as Morgan and Henry made it to the car, they called Detective McKnight to let him know that Morgan passed the polygraph.

# CHAPTER 19

Detective McKnight hated listening to stewardesses as they gave their safety speech, so he put on his headphones to drown out the thin lady in her blue uniform, along with her overly expressive gestures. He was patiently waiting until they reached 10,000 feet in the air, so that the Wi-Fi would pop back on, and he could continue listening to his jazz.

He looked over and smiled at the lady sitting next to him. It had already been a long morning after the argument he had with Shelia; she called him a bad father, because he was leaving town and not there to spend time with the boys, like he promised. He was not in the mood for small talk, so he closed his eyes and pretended to be falling sleep, hoping that the lady next to him would not try to start a conversation.

He wiggled from side to side, trying to find the right position to get comfortable in, but his knees pressed tightly against the tray on the back of the seat in front of him. Detective McKnight would usually choose his seat ahead of time, so that he could pick a spot where there was more room; but since he purchased his ticket at the last moment, he had to take whatever seat was available.

The old lady next to him whispered, "I know you are not asleep, and you look very uncomfortable. I have a neck pillow, if you want to use it." She held out a blue pillow.

He smiled and said, "No, thank you."

He turned his head and began to look out of the window; it gave him a sense of peace. The clouds brought back fond memories of him lying on the ground with the boys and imagining that the clouds were different animals. Looking out of the plane, he saw clouds in the shape of a bunny and a dog; it brought tears to his eyes...he really missed his boys. How dare Shelia call him a bad father, when he would do anything for his boys, he thought. She was the one that took them from everything that they knew and didn't even let him say goodbye.

Detective McKnight's daydreaming was interrupted by a stewardess asking if he wanted water, coffee, tea, pop, cookie, or pretzels. He declined them all.

The lady next to him elbowed him and whispered, "Get a coke and pretzels."

The stewardess laughed and handed them to him. The lady waited until the stewardess moved to the next row, and she grabbed them out of his hand.

Detective McKnight decided to listen to a new murder mystery podcast that he heard about called By Deezign Murder Mysteries. He had always been fascinated with the solving of cold cases. After all, a cold case is what motivated him to become a homicide detective.

Detective McKnight was at least grateful that he had the window seat. It was fifth time the lady sitting next to him returned from the bathroom. The pilot announced that the Wi-Fi would be turning off, and that they were about to descend. Detective McKnight went into his pocket, pulled out a piece of gum, and popped it in his mouth, hoping that chewing would alleviate any popping of his ears. He turned his head, looked out the window, and watched, as they quickly descended from the heavens, through the clouds. Everything that looked so far away started to become closer and closer.

———

Sean did not miss the blistering cold of Michigan. He called an old buddy from the academy and told him that he would be driving into Ohio the following day. He had some business he wanted to take care of in Michigan.

His friend told him that he had located Morgan Waters' father and Robin Harris, because she had not answered any of the messages that Detective McKnight had left her. He told Sean that Morgan's father was in and out of jail for disorderly conduct, usually after a long night of drinking. He also found Robin Harris; she had relapsed and was back in rehab, and she was not able to have any visitors at the moment.

It was always a bittersweet visit home. It reminded Sean of all the women that he loved and lost. His mother, grandmother, and high school sweetheart. He decided that he would stop at Coleman's. It was a local family-owned business that had been a staple of the community for as long as he could remember. Sean had fond memories going there with his grandmother. Coleman's sells fruit, veggies, flowers and some other things grown by local farmers.

He wanted to grab flowers and take them to the grave of his mother, grandmother, and Karen Lasalle. She was his high school sweetheart, who was murdered the night of their prom. Karen was the reason Sean became a detective; he wanted to solve her murder. That was his first cold case. Sean visited their graves whenever he came home to Michigan, but he had been so busy, he hadn't been to visit in a while.

He wasn't sure if it was because he was busy, or just avoidance.

Every time he came home, he was reminded of his first love and her brutal murder. It turned their small city upside down. The murder of a prom queen.

Most people have fond thoughts and feelings about their senior prom, but not Sean; his senior prom was filled with horror and sadness.

It has been over 20 years, and Sean could still see Karen's bloody, lifeless body on the ground outside the gym doors. He could vividly hear the screams and sirens. He went from being a prom king to the main suspect in her murder. Karen was the only person who truly believed in Sean, besides his grandmother.

Karen was gone, and the whole town turned on Sean. He was eventually exonerated; but by then, he lost his football scholarship, and his life was never the same.

Even after they had proof that Sean was not the murderer, people still looked at him sideways when he walked down the street. They couldn't find the actual murderer and people needed someone to blame. Even his closest friends stopped talking to him.

What hurt most of all, was when his grandmother asked him to leave and go live with his aunt. She said that she was not asking him to leave because she believed he was a murderer—she said she didn't want Sean around because she couldn't stand the pain he was going through, and how people treated him. Sean often wondered if the real reason she asked him to leave was not for his well-being, but hers.

After that, Sean moved in with his aunt. He went to Eastern Michigan University and received his bachelor's in criminal justice. At first, he was going to become an attorney. After what he experienced, he wanted to advocate for the innocent, and he thought that would be the best way to do that.

While he was in school, he started looking into Karen's death and enjoyed looking for and putting clues together, so he decided that he would become a police officer; he entered the police academy, met Shelia, got married, and they moved to Rhode Island.

Sean drove to the cemetery on Clark Road. This area was so creepy to him; he was astounded by the fact that so many people lived so close to the graveyard. As he was walking through the snow, creating a trail of footsteps behind him, his throat became tight. He started to cough, trying to relieve the pressure, but it didn't help. His eyes began to water, and he felt butterflies in his stomach.

He thought about all the what-ifs. What if Karen was never murdered? Would he have married her, instead of Shelia? Would he have had children with Karen? Would she have stood beside him through sickness and health, the good and the bad, unlike Shelia? Sean wiped the snow off of Karen's grave, only for it to be covered quickly by the rapid downfall of snow. He said a prayer and left the flowers on the grave; he made a promise to Karen that he would try to come and visit more often.

Detective McKnight eventually made it back to his rental and headed towards Ohio. It was now time for him to get to work and try to figure out who Morgan Waters really was. He turned his radio on and took 23 South, towards Toledo. He planned on driving for a few hours and then getting a hotel.

Detective McKnight wanted to pop up on Morgan's father. He found the element of surprise was often best in these situations. He stopped for the night at a Marriot, right outside of Columbus.

# CHAPTER 20

Detective McKnight had finally gotten a good night's rest; he stopped and got a coffee in the lobby before he headed out. He got into the car and entered the address of Morgan Waters' father into the GPS. He was 20 minutes away from the location.

Detective McKnight had thrown out the coffee from the lobby, because it was not strong enough and decided to stop at a Starbucks, that was right up the street. The GPS kept telling him that he was off route, so he turned it off until he was back on the road.

Detective McKnight pulled into the yard that the GPS guided him to and saw an old yellow house; there were a few shingles hanging on the front of it. It looked like it could have been a nice home, once upon a time. On the rusted fence, there was a *Beware of Dog* sign. He shook the fence, then walked into the yard. He didn't hear a dog barking...if there was one, it surely would have had met him at the gate.

As he walked up the sideway, He looked at the overgrown grass, that seemed out of place next to the neighbors nicely manicured lawns. On the side of the porch, there were cans of bud light and a red cup full of cigarette butts. Detective McKnight looked for a doorbell, but there was not one, so he knocked on the door.

A frail voice coming from behind the door said, "Who is it?"

"My name is Detective McKnight, and I have some questions to ask you about your daughter, Morgan."

"Morgan...Morgan doesn't live here. She hasn't lived here in a long time," he said.

"I know sir. Your daughter is in a lot of trouble, and I am trying to help her. Can you please come to the door?"

Detective McKnight looked over and saw the fragile man with a bald head and a peppered beard looking at him through the bay window in the living room.

"Show me your credentials." He mumbled.

Detective McKnight pulled out his badge and held it up to the window. He said, "I am a detective in Rhode Island, and I really need to ask you some questions."

Mr. Waters reluctantly opened the door and hurried Detective McKnight in, so that he would not let in the cold air.

"Have a seat. Can I get you something to drink?"

"No, I am fine. Thank you."

"So, you say my sweet Morgan is in trouble?"

"Yes sir, she is. She is a suspect in a murder investigation."

He shouted, "No, not Morgan! She has always been such a sweet and caring young lady. She had a passion for helping others and would never take another person's life. When she was a little girl, her uncle and I went hunting; we brought home a deer and some rabbit. She cried and cried. She was so upset that we had harmed those animals and refused to eat any of it, and from that day forward, she was vegan."

He stopped and looked down at the floor and then sighed, "She did change, though, when her good friend Shawna died by suicide. It was like she blamed herself. I told her that it wasn't her fault; but by that time, my words didn't mean much to Morgan. She was in college with her mind set on Law School. She has always been a very ambitious girl who didn't have much time for me...she outgrew me, I guess you could say. She did come home the night of Shawna's suicide but left the next day. That was last time she has been over here. The next time that I saw her, was when she graduated from Ohio State. A month later, she called me and told me she was moving to Rhode Island to go to law school.

Detective McKnight said, "Did Morgan ever talk to you about the road trip she took with Robin and Shawna?"

"No, she never talked about that trip, and when I would ask, she would change the subject. I had bought her a car, and when she came home, she was adamant on selling it. She said she would not need it while she was in school, and she could use the extra money that the selling the car would bring."

"Mr. Waters, I am a father; and excuse me for saying this, but if one of my kids were arrested for murder, I would be the first call that they made...but you didn't even know Morgan had been arrested. What happened between you two?"

He leaned forward and said, "Well, a lot of things happened. Morgan was only 8 years old when her mother became ill. Her chemotherapy made her very sick, and there came a point where she was too weak to get out of the bed. Morgan would sit in there with her for hours, and sometimes she would fall asleep in the chair next to her mother's bed. When she died, Morgan wouldn't leave her mother's room for days. There was nothing anyone could do to comfort her, and I wasn't the best father. After my wife died, I took up the bottle. That left little to no time for being a proper father to Morgan. A couple of times, I showed up at school events drunk; and she asked me not to come to anything anymore, so I stopped. My drinking was so bad, at one point, my brother and his wife would come over to make sure Morgan ate and got off to school. By the time she was a teenager, she was very independent. I let her do what she wanted, as long as she kept her grades up and kept the house clean."

Detective McKnight exclaimed, "Did you ever try to get Morgan any help? Did you put her in therapy?"

Pointing his finger, he yelled, "You have to understand. Detective, my wife was the glue that kept our family together. When she died, it was like our family was destroyed, and I didn't know what to do to save it. I made a lot of mistakes; but I love Morgan, even if she doesn't feel the same about me. Is there anything that I can do to help her?"

"No, thank you. I think I understand her a lot better now. You take care."

The conversation with Morgan's father woke up feelings in Detective McKnight that he had been pushing down for years. He could relate to the feeling of losing a mother at a young age. When his mother died, he was devastated; he thought his whole world had ended. His grandmother did the best she could to raise him, but she still wasn't his mother.

Detective McKnight needed to talk to his boys to reassure them of his love. He called from the car and promised his boys that as soon as he was back in town, he would get them for the weekend. He could hear Shelia's deep breaths of contempt and anger in the background.

She got on the phone and said, "I hope you keep your promise to them; the boys miss you."

He replied, "And whose fault is that, Shelia?! You took them from the only home that they have ever known, *and* from their father."

She hung up without a word. Sean decided that he would drive overnight to Tennessee; it would be less traffic, and he wanted to get there as soon as possible.

# CHAPTER 21

It was a beautiful morning; and as Detective McKnight stepped out of his car, he enjoyed the beautiful pink, red, and yellow sunrise. He wondered if his sons were up running around, and if Shelia was drinking her first cup of coffee to help her deal with those rambunctious boys.

He began to walk up to the police station. It was only one small building. He couldn't imagine where they held the inmates. The breakroom at his police station was bigger than this whole building. He couldn't wait to get out of the small town in Tennessee and get back to Rhode Island.

McKnight entered the building and walked up to the front desk. There was a young officer, who looked as if he could still be in high school, sitting behind the Post-it note-filled desk talking on his phone. Behind him was an office and two hallways: one went to the left, and the other to the right. At the end of the hallway to the right, were two cells...in one of them, there was a man who was yelling that he was innocent, and that aliens did it.

The officer looked up from his phone and exclaimed, "Good morning, Sir! How can I assist you?"

"Good morning, I'm Detective McKnight. Sheriff Walker is expecting me."

The officer knocked on the glass window behind him; and a minute later, a short, stout man, with a very deep voice walked out. He was wearing a cowboy hat with his police uniform.

"Howdy, you must be Detective McKnight. I am Sheriff Walker. It's nice to put a face with the voice."

Detective McKnight thought, *How could he chase and apprehend a suspect, if necessary, in those boots? Who am I kidding? By the looks of him, he hasn't chased anything, except maybe a meal, in years.*

"It's nice to meet you as well, Sheriff."

"Why don't you step into my office for a second? How was your drive here from Michigan?"

Detective McKnight responded, "It was ok. I made a stop in Ohio to follow a lead, and then I drove straight through. I would like to shut my eyes for a couple of hours, if I can, before we head out."

Sheriff Walker exclaimed, "You see that sofa over there? It pulls out into a nice bed! I have spent many nights on it, and not at all because I wanted to. I have an old, feisty wife, and when she gets angry with me, that sofa comes in handy. I'll be out here talking to Bo. Let me know when ya ready."

Detective McKnight laid his head on the bed and fell fast asleep. A few hours later, he was awakened by the smell of freshly baked bread. He knew that smell anywhere. His grandmother would cook it every Sunday. The thought of his grandmother brought a big smile to his face. Detective McKnight gathered himself and followed the aroma to the front desk.

Sheriff Walker said, "Have a seat. That beautiful wife of mine found out that you were in town and cooked you a meal. Let's eat before we head out."

"I'm not hungry...I would really like to get over to see Mrs. Grey's house." Detective McKnight exclaimed.

"If you refuse to eat it, will hurt my wife's feelings. Now, I know you wouldn't want to do that." Sheriff Walker scolded.

Feeling ashamed for his rude behavior, Detective McKnight agreed, "No, I wouldn't."

He took some butter and rubbed it on the warm bread. He closed his eyes and took a bite; and again, it brought back fine memories of his beloved grandmother.

Smiling, he said, "This is delicious."

Detective McKnight began wiping his bread in the gravy, and then took the last bite. He wished it wouldn't end. Not because he was still hungry, but because every bite reminded him of the happy times he had growing up; which, for him, were far and few between.

Sheriff Walker looked up from his plate and laughed and laughed saying, "Yessiree, you were not hungry at all. How about we go to see Mrs. Grey, and then go to check out Private Investigator Grey's office? I went to see his widow last night; she gave me the key to his office, and said we can have access to anything we needed, if it would help convict her husband's murderer. She is one strong lady."

Detective McKnight exclaimed, "That's great to hear."

"McKnight, is there anything that we should be looking for specifically, when we get to his office?" Sheriff Walker asked.

Detective McKnight replied, "Yes, anything about an Andre Williams, Morgan Waters, Shawna Smith, or Robin Harris. We should also keep an eye out for anything involving a hit and run of a young man, that happened in 2005."

Sheriff Walker turned beet red and bemoaned, "That is my cold case! I will never forget the night that poor young man was hit, and then thrown aside like a piece of trash. That's the case that keeps me up at night. I never knew that Private Investigator Grey was hired to work that case."

"Sheriff, what was the name of the young man who died, and what do you remember about the case?"

Sheriff Walker replied, "His name was Jeremy Knotts. He was 15 years old, and the pride and joy of the town. He was the starting quarterback at the local high school—that was quite a feat for a freshman to be the starter on a varsity football team in this town. That night, the team had just won the division championship. Jeremy went to the gas station to get some snacks, and never made it back home. It is sad...so sad. A few years after he died, his mother died. I think it was from a broken heart; it was only her and Jeremy."

Sheriff Walker began pointing his finger and lamented, "That's the road where it happened, right there."

The Sheriff slammed on the brakes, and did a quick U-turn in the middle of the deserted road. He slowed the car down to a halt, then stepped out.

He walked over to the edge of the road, and Detective McKnight closely followed.

Sheriff McKnight removed his hat and sighed, "This is where we found him...right there. He was in the ditch and had some leaves thrown over him. We always suspected that it was someone from out of town, maybe a spectator at the game that night. We did receive a phone call from the pay phone up the street, that alerted us that he was in the ditch. The caller was anonymous, but it was somebody with a little conscience. The officer who took the call, said that the young lady who called could have been a teenager. We had no witnesses and no leads...the case quickly went cold."

# CHAPTER 22

Detective McKnight and Sheriff Walker walked back to the car and quietly rode to Private Investigator Grey's home. They pulled into a driveway that seemed to go on for a mile. It was a very narrow road, that had a couple of sharp turns. Detective McKnight was convinced that they didn't have many guests on regular basis, because there would be no way for a car to be coming and leaving at the same time. One of the cars would have to give in and back up to a wider space, to allow the other car to pass by.

They finally made it in the house. Sheriff Walker was clearly used to the long, slender, curvy driveways and hopped right out of the car. Detective McKnight, a bit unnerved, slowly stepped out of the car and walked up to the door.

The shades were pulled tight, and it seemed as though there was no movement going on inside. Sheriff Walker did confirm that it was Mrs. Grey's green sedan in the driveway.

The Sheriff knocked and knocked and then said, "Mrs. Grey, it's Sheriff Walker and Detective McKnight, from Rhode Island."

Finally, they heard a shaky voice through the door that said, "I'll be right with you."

Mrs. Grey answered the door. She was pale and her eyes were puffy. She was wearing a yellow sundress, and was tying on an apron.

She whispered, "I'm sorry I took so long to answer the door, I was napping...you actually startled me. Would you like coffee or tea?"

Sheriff Walker said, "Yes, we would both have coffee."

Mrs. Grey led them to her family room, and they sat down on her floral couch that was covered in plastic, as she went to the kitchen to grab the drinks.

When she returned to the room, Detective McKnight said, "I'm so sorry about the death of your husband. We are working tirelessly to solve the case. We have a suspect in custody who has confessed, but we are trying to figure out his motive in order to solidify the prosecutor's case."

Her eyes filling with tears, as she cried, "Thank you! This has been horrible. I don't know what I am going to do without Johnny. He was my everything. We would have been celebrating our 30th anniversary this month. He was such a wonderful man, who dedicated his life to others. Did you know that is why he became a PI? All he wanted to do was help others."

Sheriff Walker got up and sat next to Mrs. Grey, put his arm around her, and pulled her close saying, "I am so sorry, Ma'am."

"I need to ask you a few questions right now. Have you ever heard your husband talk about an Andre Williams?" Detective McKnight said.

"No, that name does not sound familiar."

Following up with another question, he asked, "Do you know if he was investigating the hit and run of Jeremy Knotts?"

She sat up straight and said, "Yes, Johnny was obsessed with the case, ever since that poor boy's mother hired him to try to find the driver of the car that hit her son. Any time Johnny had a new lead, he would follow it. Sometimes years would go by, and he would not work the case, and then something or someone would make him start looking all over again. I told Johnny...I told him this case would be the death of him."

Detective McKnight said, "Why would you say that?"

"Johnny told me that he thought he uncovered something else while searching for the hit and run driver. He never told me what it was. He did say, though, that if anyone ever came by, to tell them nothing. He received a strange phone call a couple of weeks ago, with someone demanding that he come forward with the information that he had. He told them, "No," and that Ms. Knotts was the only person privy to the information he gathered, and she had died. He told them if he did figure anything out, he would be bringing that information to the police."

Sheriff Walker asked, "Did it seem like he knew the person?"

"I'm not sure. Maybe?"

Detective McKnight asked, "Mrs. Grey, did your husband tell you why he was traveling to Rhode Island?"

"No, but I do know he started working the case again, and for the last few months had been going out of town almost every weekend. Johnny had been a private investigator for a long time; I stopped asking years ago where he was going."

Sheriff Walker took one more sip from his coffee, stood up, and said, "Okay; well, thank you, ma'am. Do you have any other questions for her, Detective?"

"No, thank you for your time, ma'am; and again, I am so sorry for your loss." Detective McKnight said.

# Chapter 23

Detective McKnight walked away from the conversation with Mrs. Grey reassured that he was on to something. They headed down the skinny, curvy road towards Private Investigator Johnathan Grey's office.

It looked more like a shack, than an office. The siding that was now hanging off the building was discolored. One of his windows had wood over it, and the grass was overgrown. On the outside, there was a handmade sign that said *Johnathan Grey Private Investigator*.

Mrs. Grey told Johnny that he could not put money into fixing up his office until they finished the renovations on their home, so he improvised and always met prospective clients at the local diner.

When they walked inside, Detective McKnight was distracted by all the clutter. There were files and papers everywhere. When training new detectives, he always told them it was important to keep their desk clean. He always told them, "A cluttered desk leads to a cluttered mind," and that the job was difficult enough; they didn't need to add any unnecessary obstacles, because a detective needed a clear mind to figure things out.

Detective McKnight walked over to the file cabinet that was behind Grey's desk, while Sheriff Walker began opening the desk drawers and looking at the papers that were sitting on the desk.

Detective McKnight was pulling out files, when he noticed a manila folder all the way in the back of the cabinet drawer. He opened it up, and inside was an envelope. On the outside, it said *Morgan Waters and Andre Williams.* Detective McKnight's eyes bulged from his head. He was not ready to share with Sheriff Walker the information that he knew about Morgan.

He looked around to make sure the sheriff was not looking; he put the envelop in the pocket on the inside of his coat and continued to look through the filing cabinet.

After a few hours of searching, they headed to the local diner for dinner. Saturday's special was meatloaf and mashed potatoes.

They ate and talked about their law enforcement careers. Once they finished, they headed to the police station, so that Detective McKnight could pick up his car and head to the hotel for the night. Detective McKnight began to feel guilty for hiding the envelop, but he had to know what was in the envelope, and he wasn't ready to reveal anything before he knew his next move.

They said goodnight, and Detective McKnight hurried to his car. He was anticipating what could be in the envelope. *Was it Andre's true identity? Did Private Investigator Grey have some incriminating information about Morgan? Would this be the piece of the puzzle missing to understand why Andre murdered Private Investigator Grey?*

Detective McKnight held his phone up to the sensor on his hotel door. The red light started flashing; he pulled the phone back and tried again...a smile went across his face when the green light flashed, and he was able to open the door. He threw his backpack and jacket on the bed, then loosened his tie and unbuttoned his blue dress shirt, revealing his ironed, white t-shirt underneath.

He reached into his jacket pocket and pulled the envelop out.

He slowly began to open it, to ensure that he would not destroy any evidence that might be inside.

He was surprised to see a bunch of pictures in the envelope. He began to pull them out one by one. There were photos of both Morgan and Andre. It appeared that Private Investigator Grey had been following them for a while.

He sat the pictures on the bed and pulled out a news article that was folded up in the envelope. The story was about a young lady who had been found raped and murdered in 2004. The article said she was visiting her family in Tennessee; she was from Mississippi. It went on to say that forensics had found two sets of DNA on her clothing. All of law enforcement's leads had gone cold after that.

Many people thought that the case hadn't been diligently pursued, because the victim was a young, African American girl. A local activist mentioned in the story the disparity in the quality of investigations by the police when the victim is a person of color vs. when the victim was white.

The activist was right. The precinct had brought in a specialist on that very topic in Rhode Island. They were looking to start a new incentive; many of Detective McKnight's coworkers declined to attend. They felt that they had enough on their plates, and many of them were tired of all the recent policy changes in the department. Detective McKnight went, because it was a concern of his.

The article said that the young woman was found in a dumpster behind a local arcade in a small town named Kinsee; it also said that there were no cooperating witnesses. Written in bold letters on the top of the article, was the name "Bryan Simmons."

This piqued Detective McKnight's interest, so he called Sheriff Walker to see if he could get the case file on the murder of the young lady. He told Sheriff Walker that he had just read an article about her rape and murder, and that he had experience solving cold cases. After all, he had solved the murder of his high school sweetheart several years ago. Something in his gut was telling him that the case may have something to do with the murder of Private Investigator Grey.

Ten minutes later, Detective McKnight's phone rang.

"Howdy, McKnight, this is Sheriff Walker. I had Bo fetch you that case file...you can pick it up tomorrow," he exclaimed.

The next morning, Detective McKnight went to the police station, and Sheriff Walker had the file ready for him. Sheriff Walker told Detective McKnight that he remembered the case and to call him if he had any questions.

Detective McKnight nodded his and headed to the airport.

# CHAPTER 24

Morgan was running through the airport, so she would not miss her plane. She had told Mr. Calloway she wanted to go back home for the weekend and relax. It had been a few days since she had been alone. There was always either the Calloways around, or the policeman who had been assigned as her escort. Morgan knew that she could not tell Mr. Calloway that she was going to Ohio. He would not have approved of it. Especially since one of the conditions of her being released, was that she did not leave town.

Morgan bumped into a mother, who was rocking her baby to sleep; she apologized as she began to slow down, because her gate was next. Morgan plopped down in an empty seat and set her bag on the next chair, between her and a young boy, who had his headphones in and was oblivious that she was there. She leaned her head back and exhaled; relieved that they had not started to board the plane yet.

She turned to reach into her bag, when she saw Detective McKnight exiting a plane. Morgan's heart began to pound, and she looked around to see if she could find somewhere to hide, so that he would not see her. She pulled up her hood and turned towards the window.

She knew if he saw her, he would force her to leave the airport. Although he had been very kind, she could not take the chance that he would arrest her for not obeying the conditions of her release.

Morgan grabbed her foundation out of her purse and pretended to powder her nose. She held her arm out and lifted the mirror, so that she could watch until Detective McKnight passed by. She heard the attendant call for first class, and she grabbed her bag and quickly moved towards the line. With a sigh of relief, Morgan held her phone out to scan her ticket and walked onto the plane.

# CHAPTER 25

Detective McKnight went straight to his office from the airport. He pulled out the pictures, spread them out on his desk, and carefully examined each one. He switched his attention from the pictures and began rereading the article about the young lady who had been raped and murdered. *Why did Private Investigator Grey have the name "Bryan Simmons" written on the top of the article?* he thought.

Detective McKnight laid his head back on his chair and sat the paper down; he began to rub his brow. Sitting himself back up, he glanced again at the article and noticed that there were three numbers written really small on the bottom of the article: 328. He had paid so much attention to the name written at the top, that he hadn't noticed the numbers before.

The detective picked up his phone and called Sheriff Walker.

"Hey, Sheriff, I was wondering if I could get the number for PI Grey's wife? I may be on to something."

"Howdy, McKnight! I sure do. Would you like to share whatcha thinking?"

"Not yet, Sheriff, but if I find anything out, you will be my first call."

"Ok, McKnight, I'll be talking to ya soon, and hopefully you will have something to share."

Detective McKnight drank down his last bit of coffee and then picked up his phone.

"Hello, Mrs. Grey, this is Detective McKnight."

She replied, "Hello, Detective, I usually don't answer calls when I don't recognize the number, but something told me to pick up."

"Thank you, ma'am. I am happy that you did. I was wondering if you could give me any insight into something. I was going through some of your husband's things, and I ran across the number, 328. Does that mean anything to your husband?

Mrs. Grey gasped and said, "That was the day our beautiful daughter Liza died! She was eight years old, and one day she came home from school with a fever, stiff neck, and a severe headache. We took her to the hospital, and they said she had meningitis. She passed away a week later. Life is never the same when you lose a child. Now I no longer have Liza or Johnny."

"I am awfully sorry, ma'am."

"Thank you...Johnny often used that date for his passwords, and he also used it as the code to our lock box with all of our important documents. He said that was the day his life changed forever."

"Ma'am, would you mind going to grab that box?"

"Sure, Detective, do you think that there is something in there that could help you find out why my Johnny was murdered?"

"To be honest, I don't know. I have a gut feeling that your husband was on to something big, and I am trying to follow his clues. I am not sure what I am looking for, but I will know it when I find it."

Mrs. Grey walked quickly down the hall, stepping over a pile of clothes she was going through to donate. She opened her bedroom door and lifted up the floral bed sheet that hung to the floor. She stuck her hand under the bed and moved her arm, around until she felt the container. She pulled it toward her and ran back up the hall to the phone.

Breathing heavily, she said, "Ok, Detective, I have it."

"Ok, great! Can you look through it and see if any documents are missing, or if there is anything in there that you don't recognize? It could be a piece a paper with dates that are not familiar, names that you have never heard before, anything that you see that shouldn't be in with your personal documents."

Mrs. Grey began to rummage through the container. She picked up a picture with her, Liza, and Johnny. As she held the picture close to her heart, a tear ran down her face. She set the picture softly on the table and continued to look through the lock box.

She said, "Wait, one minute. There is a lock of hair in here. It's not mine, Johnathan's, or Liza's...we are all brunettes, and this hair is blonde."

"Ma'am, I am going to have Sheriff Walker come and pick that lock of hair up from you, ok?"

She replied, "Ok."

Detective McKnight called Sheriff Walker and asked him to go to Mrs. Grey's home and pick up the lock of hair that she had found in their lock box. He couldn't tell Sheriff Walker the truth; that he uncovered the information from evidence that he found in Private Investigator Grey's office. Evidence that he had concealed.

Detective McKnight had never done anything like that before, but he believed Morgan, when she said that she had nothing to do with the murder; and he was not ready to share any information with the authorities in Tennessee or with District Attorney Hughes that could potentially incriminate her.

Detective McKnight looked at the clock and tossed everything into his satchel. It was time for him to pick the boys up from school. He was looking forward to his time with them. He called the forensic lab on the way to his car, to let Nita know that some evidence was being sent to her from Tennessee, and it needed to be a priority.

# CHAPTER 26

S ean watched as all the kids streamed out of the elementary school yelling and running. As they reached the buses, most of the kids conformed and lined up neatly, waiting to get on the bus. There was a small group of students who chased each other as the teacher tried to get them to stand in line. After a few attempts of unsuccessfully trying to get the students to conform, the teacher stepped back and allowed them to continue playing tag.

A huge smile came across Sean's face, as he saw his boys running towards his car. He got out of the car and began to head towards them. Right behind the boys, was a tall, brunette school administrator with glasses and her hair pulled back into a bun walking close behind the boys, making sure they were running towards an adult approved to pick them up. As she walked closer and recognized Sean, she smiled and allowed the boys to continue to run towards him.

"Daddy! Daddy! Daddy!" they yelled, as they ran closer to him, with their arms out.

Sean bent down on one knee and opened his arms. He pulled his sons toward him and held them close. He gave them each a kiss on the check and rubbed their heads, as they walked back towards the car.

In the car, the boys went on about the new place they lived in, and how they like their old house better. They asked when they could come back home. With every word, Sean's heart broke a little more.

He said, "Boys, I know you miss me. I miss you too. Just always remember that no matter where we live, daddy loves you very much."

He looked in the rear-view mirror and said, "Guess what we are having for dinner? PIZZA!!"

The boys threw their hands in the air in celebration. The somber looks on their faces turned into smiles.

They made it home, and Sean ordered the boys' favorite pizza: ham and pineapple. He sat with the oldest two boys, as they worked on their homework, while his youngest ran around with a dinosaur, growling.

Sean wanted to keep the boys overnight, but Shelia said the therapist felt it was too soon, and it would confuse them. She wanted the boys to get used to the new place and not think that they were moving back. Sean didn't know if it was the therapist or Shelia, but he was going to make sure he made it to the boys' next session, so he would know for sure.

They ate pizza, drank juice, and had ice cream. Sean took the boys to the park to play. They ran, swung, and watched the clouds, calling out the different animals as they appeared. The park was filled by their laughs and smiles. Sean didn't want the day to end.

Sean sighed, "Boys, we have to go back to the house and get your things together, so I can take you to your mom's."

They begged to stay with him longer, but he knew how Shelia was about their bedtimes. Even though Sean's heart ached to do it, he got them in the car, picked up their things, and drove them to Shelia's new home.

# CHAPTER 27

After dropping the boys off at Shelia's, Detective McKnight decided to go back to his office and set some fire up under Nita. He needed to know who that hair belonged to. He fell back into his brown, leather chair and twirled his favorite pen around in his hand. It was the cheesy gift that your jobs give you for putting up with their crap for five years. His ten-year gift was a coffee mug and a plaque.

He really wished that he still had his boys with him. Not having a father in his life, Detective McKnight knew how important his presence in his sons' lives was.

His phone rang. He looked down, and it was Nita.

"Hey, McKnight, this is Nita."

"Hello, Ms. Nita. I was about to give you a call."

"I know how impatient you are, McKnight, so I called as soon as I got a hit on the DNA. The hair belongs to a Jeremy Knotts. He was a victim of a hit and run in Tennessee back in 2005. How did you get your hands on a sample of hair from someone who has been dead for so long?"

"I can't go into it now, Nita. I will explain it all to you over that steak and scotch that I owe you. Thank you, Ms. Nita! I'll be talking to you soon," He exclaimed.

"Goodbye, good looking," Nita whispered.

As soon as he hung up with Nita, he called Sheriff Walker.

"Hey, Sheriff, I hope I haven't caught you at a bad time."

"Howdy, McKnight, you caught me just about to sit for a quick dinner with the Missus."

"I have an update on the case; I am still not sure what it means, but the hair we found in Grey's lock box belonged to Jeremy Knotts!" he exclaimed.

"Well I'll be...why would PI Grey have Jeremy Knotts' hair?"

"I'm not sure what's going on, Sheriff, but I must say it is bizarre that he would be holding on to a lock of Jeremy's hair," he said.

I replied, "I'm not sure why he would have Jeremy's hair, but this case is becoming more and more weird. Every time we find out something new, it brings a whole new dynamic. I am confident that the answer to all of this is in Tennessee."

Sheriff Walker exclaimed, "McKnight, it might be worth you making another trip here."

Detective McKnight said, "I was thinking the same thing. Let me bring my captain up to date on all of these new developments, and see if she will approve me coming back out there for a day or so."

---

"Thank you, Sheriff Walker for meeting me today."

"My pleasure, McKnight."

"By the way, thank you. My captain told me you called her, and was pretty convincing on why I should come back to visit."

Chuckling, the Sheriff said, "I've been doing this a long time, McKnight, and I have learned that with a dab of charm and the art of convincing a person that they came up with my brilliant idea on their own, gets 'em every time. You city folk call it reverse psychology."

Smiling, Detective McKnight said, "Sheriff, when this case is over, I'm going to need you to teach me how you do it. But for right now, as far as you know, was there any relationship between the Grey family and the Knott family before Private Investigator Grey was hired to look into Jeremy's murder?"

Sheriff Walker pulled a handkerchief out of his back pocket to wipe his brow and said, "No, the Knott's family have been in the town for as long back as the town existed. In fact, Jeremy's great, great, great grandfather was one of the founders. The Grey family moved here maybe one year before Jeremy died. I believe they came here after they lost their daughter."

"Maybe Ms. Knott's gave it to Mr. Grey to match, if he ever found any forensic evidence in the case." Detective McKnight said.

"You are not just a handsome fella. You are smart. I guess that's why you are the big city detective." They both laughed.

Sheriff Walker said, "I started thinking after you left about the young woman who was raped and murdered. When we caught that case. I was a young officer, and the Sheriff at that time, was not too concerned about a "dead black gal." Those were his words. We asked a few questions, but we never thoroughly investigated. Then, the following year, Jeremy Knotts was hit and killed, and the young lady's death no longer mattered to anyone...except for her aunt. She would come weekly for updates, and we would tell her we had no news for her. The truth was, we were not looking. Maybe we should go talk to this aunt?"

# CHAPTER 28

"Hello, Ms. Kingston."

"Hello, Sheriff."

"Ms. Kingston, this is Detective McKnight, from Rhode Island; we are here regarding the unsolved rape and murder of your niece. Ma'am, we would like to ask you a few questions, if you don't mind."

She sneered, "If I don't mind! I have been coming to that police station every year and no one cares! No one cared about a poor black girl being killed, so what makes y'all care now? Do you know how many sleepless nights I have had? How I've imagined all the horrific things that my niece endured? I play it over and over and over again in my head. I think about the people who did this to her; they are probably sleeping with no problem. If you being here means that someone will listen, that someone realizes that my niece's life matters, that her death matters—then, yes, I'll answer whatever questions that you have."

Looking her straight in her eyes, Detective McKnight said, "Ma'am, I'm so sorry that you and your family have had no closure.

I hope that we are able to bring that to you now. I promise you that I will personally look into her murder!"

She said with a sniffle, "Her name is Kasey. She was the sweetest and most caring girl. She would always come into my room in the morning with a great big smile on her face. She would climb into my bed to give me a hug and a kiss on my cheek, and to tell me how much she loved me."

Detective McKnight said, "Thank you, ma'am, for sharing a little about Kasey with us. Can you tell me anything that you remember about the night that Kasey was murdered?"

Ms. Kingston sat back in her chair and replied, "Yes, I remember it like yesterday. I often wonder if I could have done or said something different that night; maybe she would still be here. Kasey came here to visit every summer, since she was two years old. She loved coming here, because I have three children of my own, so she had people to play with. She was my sister's only child. You know my sister never recovered...she died three years ago from cancer, without any answers."

"I am so sorry," Detective McKnight bemoaned.

Ms. Kingston said, "That night, my daughter, son, my son's best friend, and Kasey went to the arcade downtown. The girls wanted to go alone, but I insisted that the boys go with them to keep them safe. My daughter said that they were in the arcade playing Skee-ball, and Kasey said she had to go to the bathroom. When my daughter looked up, Kasey was heading outside. After a few minutes, my daughter decided that she was going to go outside and look for Kasey. She found her talking to some boy. Kasey told my daughter not to say anything to my son, because he would not have had any of that. My daughter said about 30 minutes went by, and Kasey had not come back in, so she went and found her brother and they went outside looking for Kasey. They found her in the back laying on top of the trash in the dumpster. They threw her away like trash..."

Ms. Kingston was sitting in her recliner with her hands

covering her face crying. Detective McKnight and Sheriff Walker looked at each other. Sheriff Walker shaking his head. He was ashamed of himself, because he knew that when it happened, law enforcement didn't work on the case as hard as they should have.

Detective McKnight said, "I know how it feels to lose someone in such a horrible way and not to have answers. Can I give you a hug?"

She smiled and said, "Yes, you can, young man."

As Detective McKnight was hugging her, he caught a glimpse of a picture that made his heart begin to race. He stood up straight, pointing at the picture, as he walked towards it to get a closer look.

Detective McKnight exclaimed, "Ma'am, who is this right here in this picture?"

Pulling her glasses up, that were hanging around her neck attached to a string of pearls, onto her eyes she said, "Oh, that is my son's old friend, Bryan...Bryan Simmons."

Sheriff Walker said, "Ma'am, was Bryan the friend that went along the night of the murder?"

She replied, "Yes!"

Detective McKnight said, "Excuse me, ma'am, I need to have a word with the Sheriff really fast."

They stepped outside, and Detective McKnight blurted out, "She knows him as Bryan Simmons...I know him as Andre Williams!! He is the man who is sitting in jail in Rhode Island right now charged with murdering Private Investigator Johnathan Grey."

Sheriff Walker said, "What!! Do you think he murdered Kasey?"

Without hesitation, Detective McKnight exclaimed, "Without a doubt!"

Detective McKnight and Sheriff Walker walked back into the house and over to Ms. Kingston.

Detective McKnight grabbed Ms. Kingston's hand and said, "Ma'am, you have helped us more than you know. I will be getting in contact with you soon."

She said patting his hand, "Thank you! Thank you, both!"

Detective McKnight and Sheriff Walker walked back to the patrol car deep in thought. Sheriff Walker stopped by the car and looked up at the sky. It was a beautiful night and the stars were lighting up the sky. He could not help but to think that if they had worked harder to solve Kasey's murder, then maybe Mrs. Grey would not be mourning the loss of her husband. He said a quick prayer and then got into the car.

Detective McKnight said, "Sheriff, are you ok?"

"McKnight, it is always that one case that keeps you up at night. This is mine. I knew we didn't do right by this family, but I was just a deputy then; I was just following orders."

Detective McKnight put his hands on Sheriff Walker's shoulder and said, "You're a good man, Sheriff, and you can't change any of that; but how about we give the family some closure now."

Sheriff Walker said, "Well, since our cases are connected for sure, I would love to help you get enough evidence to throw that piece of trash in jail for the rest of his miserable life."

Detective McKnight said, "Do you still have the evidence from Kasey's murder?"

"Yes, we keep all the cold case files in the basement at the station."

Not wanting to waste any time getting back to the police station Sheriff Walker flipped a switch, and the sirens and lights on his car turned on. He drove through the back roads as fast as he could; he knew them like the back of his hand and could drive them with his eyes closed. Sheriff grew up in the town, and there was not a curve in the road that he was not aware of. Holding on to the car door handle, Detective McKnight closed his eyes; he was sure that they would end up in a ditch.

Detective McKnight followed closely behind Sheriff Walker, as they descended down the narrow staircase. He reached out for a non-existent handrail, then asked Sheriff Walker who the genius was that came up with the idea of having the light switch at the bottom of the stairs. Sheriff Walker said that he complained about it many times, but the higher powers refused to have an electrician add an outlet at the top of the stairs. They claimed that they couldn't justify the cost. Especially, since all that was stored in the basement were the cold cases; and nobody ever worked them.

Sheriff Walker said, "You'll be fine, Detective, I promise. I haven't lost anyone yet, bringing them down here."

Sheriff Walker flicked on the light. Detective McKnight looked around and saw file cabinets and dusty boxes everywhere.

He said, "Hopefully, there is some type of filing system down here. I'm not ready for another scavenger hunt."

Sheriff Walker replied, "Yes, we have a system. Everything is labeled by the year. This murder took place in 2004. He started looking at the boxes: 2001, 2002...Here we go, 2004! I'm sure this is the box."

Detective McKnight said, "Let's pray that we have the DNA that they found, to run against Andre Williams...I mean Bryan Simmons."

Sheriff Walker began to rub his chin and said, "McKnight... I just had a really disturbing thought. Maybe we should run both Bryan Simmons and Jeremy Knotts' DNA."

Sitting the box back down, Detective McKnight said, "Sheriff, you may be on to something."

Wiping off all the dust from his shirt, Sheriff Walker opened the box and began carefully looking through it. After a moment, he shouted, "Here they are!! Here are the samples! I hope those fancy forensics folks you have up there in the big city are able to get something from them."

Detective McKnight sighed, "I hope so too."

# CHAPTER 29

Sitting in the Calloway's living room, Morgan watched the flames and enjoyed the smell of the embers from the fireplace. She was hoping that her trip to Ohio, to visit her old friend Robin Harris, would not come back and cause her more legal problems.

The visit brought back so many bad memories. Morgan had not been back there since she left for law school. On her way back to the airport, she had her Uber driver take her past her old home. It didn't look the same as she remembered. She wondered if her father was inside passed out, like he was most nights, when she was growing up.

Tears began to stream down her face as she thought about her mother. Then, she began to rub her wrist, feeling her bracelet. It was her mother's dream for her to become a lawyer. Even though Morgan's dream had always been to be a model, with the hope of one day appearing on America's Next Top Model, she become a lawyer; just like she promised her mom, the night before she passed away.

Morgan had made many mistakes that she regretted, but she

knew that her mother would have been so proud of her. She would like to think that her father was too, but the only thing he had cared about for years was his next drink.

Morgan began to take deep breaths. Just thinking about all that she went through, because of her father, filled her with uncontrollable anger. She hurled the glass of wine that she was drinking towards the fireplace, and she watched the shards of glass fly everywhere. Teenage Morgan would have grabbed those shards and cut her arm or inner thigh, to relive the pain. Instead, she began to snap her bracelet, waiting for the overwhelming sensation to harm herself to leave.

Mrs. Calloway heard the commotion and ran into the living room. She could see the pain in Morgan's eyes. Morgan fell back on the couch and apologized for breaking the glass.

Mrs. Calloway sat next to her, and putting her arms around Morgan, she whispered, "Morgan, everything will be ok. Don't worry about the glass I'll clean it—Maybe you should go lie down and rest."

Morgan smiled at Mrs. Calloway. Without saying a word, she got up and headed towards the guest bedroom.

# CHAPTER 30

"Good evening, McKnight, this is your favorite forensic tech, Nita. I got your message. Don't send me the samples; I know I can't get them back to you as quickly as you need them. I called a friend from the FBI who has had a crush on me since we met at a molecular genetics' seminar. I have to go out on a date with him, but he said if we get the samples to him by morning, he should have results back within 12 hours. It shouldn't be that difficult, since we have DNA to compare the samples too."

"Nita, you are heaven sent. I owe you big...text me his information."

"Done! McKnight, you sound like you are exhausted; go get you some rest."

Sighing, he said, "After I get these samples sent out, I promise I will try and do that."

"Sheriff, do you have anywhere close by where we can have these samples sent out overnight?" Detective McKnight asked.

"Not here, but in the town next to us, they have a FedEx. It's about a 45-minute drive."

McKnight smirked and said, "Well, I'm sure if you put those sirens and lights on again, you can have us there in 20."

———

After getting back from dropping off the samples to be sent to the FBI, Detective McKnight decided he should call his Captain to get her all caught up on the new evidence. Even though it was late, he knew that she would want him to call her. She was reluctant in letting him go; it's an election year, so every department's budget was under review. If Detective McKnight came back empty-handed again, she didn't want to have to explain to the chief why one of her detectives went to Tennessee twice in one week, with no evidence to help the case.

Detective McKnight finished his conversation with the captain; she was very pleased. She told him that he could bring District Attorney Hughes up to date when he received the DNA results.

Detective McKnight got off the phone and laid back on the bed; he folded his arms behind his head and crossed his legs. He took a deep breath in, then exhaled slowly. He could barely keep his eyes opened. He fell fast asleep; this was the first time since the case started that he was able to get a full night's rest.

Detective McKnight was awoken by a loud knock on the door. Wiping his eyes, he sat up, went to the door, and looked out of the peep hole. Standing there with a bag in one hand, and a tray with two coffees in the other, was Sheriff Walker. Detective McKnight opened the door.

"It took you long enough to come to the door, McKnight. I thought that I would send you off right. I brought you fresh donuts from the town's famous bakery and a cup of coffee. This is what I eat to maintain my fine physique."

Laughing, Detective McKnight said, "Sheriff, you are one of a kind! Thank you."

"Let's get going. I'll give you an escort to the airport. I promised your captain that I would not keep you a day longer than necessary, and I am a man of my word," he said, as he took a bite from his chocolate donut with sprinkles.

# CHAPTER 31

Nita ran to her phone; it was on the other side of the lab. She left it next to some specimens she was testing for a double homicide case. She kept promising herself that she was going to take off those 15 pounds that she gained from her last breakup. She only noticed the extra pounds when she moved quickly, or when she tried to button up a pair of blue jeans.

Panting, she picked up her phone and said, "Hello, Special Agent Franklin."

"Hello, Nita, how is your day going?"

"It's going ok! It would be better if you were calling with those DNA results."

"I am, even though most of the evidence had been exposed to the elements, and I was not able to pull anything from them. However, I was able to find enough DNA to make two positive matches. I don't know if it is enough to hold up in court; both suspects were in our database. One matched to a felon named Bryan Simmons, and the other matched to Jeremy Knotts...he was a new cold case that a file was recently started on."

Nita exclaimed, "Thank you so much! I have to go and call the detective working this case."

Nita hung up before Special Agent Franklin could ask her about the date she promised him. She found Sean's name in her contacts and called him. Then, she heard a knock on her door, and standing there with a coffee in his hand was Detective McKnight.

She looked down at her phone, and a smile grew across her face, "I was just about to call you."

"I was antsy, so I decided I would keep you company while you wait to hear from your FBI boyfriend."

Nita pushed him playfully and said, "Ha, ha, ha...you got jokes. I have the results, Sean. The DNA belongs to Bryan Simmons and Jeremy Knotts."

Sean replied, "WHAT!! I was 100% positive that one of the samples would be Bryan Simmons, but Jeremy Knotts? Whoaaaa...I have to make a call."

He left the room and went to the hallway to call Sheriff Walker.

"Hey, Sheriff, you were right. We got them! The DNA matched Jeremy Knotts and Andre Williams. Did you know that they knew each other?"

He replied, "No, I figured that they would both be about the same age, and Jeremy was from the same town, but I was hoping I was wrong."

Detective McKnight began to feel bad for keeping the secret about Morgan and her friends. He decided to tell Sheriff Walker everything.

"Sheriff, I have to tell you something. The day we were searching Private Investigator Grey's office, I found an envelope and in it was pictures of the two suspects in my murder investigation. I couldn't tell you, because I don't believe that one of the suspects, Morgan Waters, had anything to do with Grey's murder. However, she did admit to me that she was a passenger in the car that killed Jeremy Knotts. I feel bad that I kept it from you, but I didn't know if I could trust you with that information at the time."

"Well, McKnight, I guess I've earned your trust now, 'cause you're telling me all this, and you didn't have too. You put your career on the line for Ms. Waters. I'll tell you something else, I know you folks in the big city have to be politically correct about everything, but I don't have any problem saying what I think. As far as I am concerned, Ms. Waters and her friends performed a public service. Too bad that rascal you have in custody now wasn't crossing the street with Jeremy. Now we have a new, very ambitious District Attorney here, so I can't say that she will feel the same. I'm sure she is going to want to talk to Ms. Waters"

"I understand; I know the type. Do you think you could hold off on telling her just for a couple of days? I want to interview Andre...I mean Bryan, and see what else we can get from him."

"McKnight, I have no problem with that; under one condition. You let me come out to Rhode Island with you, so I can look evil in the eyes and see his face, when he knows that he is going to fry."

Detective McKnight sighed, "Sheriff, we don't have the death penalty in Rhode Island."

He bellowed, "No, but we have it here in good ole Tennessee. Maybe we can see if our ambitious DAs can work together and have him extradited. Then, maybe we can give my District Attorney here a bigger case; she will be more lenient on Ms. Waters."

Detective McKnight exclaimed, "Pack your bags my friend!"

# CHAPTER 32

Before Detective McKnight went to pick up Sheriff Walker from the airport, he stopped by District Attorney Hughes' office to bring him up to date on all the new evidence. He told DA Hughes about the DNA evidence that connects Andre Williams a.k.a Bryan Simmons, to an unsolved rape and murder of a 16-year-old girl in Tennessee, back in 2004.

It aggravated Detective McKnight, because it seemed like District Attorney Hughes was excited about this information. You could see DA Hughes' eyes light up like stars in the sky. All he could see was the publicity, which was always a good thing in an election year. Detective McKnight didn't share any information with him regarding Morgan's role in all of this, in fear that it would blur District Attorney Hughes' focus on Bryan Simmons.

Detective McKnight felt both an overwhelming sadness, because it took so long to get justice for Kasey's family; and anger, because if she was not a person of color, more effort would have been put into solving her case by law enforcement. He looked forward to seeing the relief and closure from the family, when they tell them that they finally will have justice for Kasey.

CHAPTER 32

District Attorney Hughes told Detective McKnight that he had a meeting that he was already late for, but he would contact Bryan Simmons's attorney and set up a time to meet. Detective McKnight asked DA Hughes if he would be available in a couple of hours to talk more. They agreed to meet back up, and Detective McKnight walked out towards his car.

As Detective McKnight headed towards the airport, he passed the boys' school and wondered how their day was going. He hadn't talk to them, and he missed them dearly. He wanted to call Shelia and tell her that he would agree to anything she wanted, as long as he had joint legal and physical custody of the boys.

Not knowing when he would be able to see his boys was not okay with him. He never wanted his sons to experience what he had growing up; feeling unwanted and unloved by his father.

Detective McKnight pulled up at Delta's pickup area, and walking out of the sliding doors, he saw his new friend in his brown cowboy hat, leather vest, and brown cowboy boots. He stood outside the car, pulled his sunglasses down, and waved his arm. A huge grin spread across Sheriff Walker's face, and he walked over to the car.

"Howdy, McKnight! Thanks for picking me up. I thought that maybe I would have to catch one of those Ubers you folks have up here. It never made much sense to me hopping into a car with a complete stranger."

Detective McKnight opened his trunk, grabbed Sheriff Walker's luggage from him and tossed them in. Then he pulled his sunglasses back down, checked his rear-view mirror, and pulled out; heading back to talk to District Attorney Hughes.

Detective McKnight and DA Hughes both pulled in at the same time. Detective McKnight introduced Sheriff Walker to Hughes; the growing tension between the DA and Detective was obvious.

Sheriff Walker said, "I see you fellas have a few things to talk about. I saw a nice hotdog stand up the street, that I think I'm gonna try. Would either of you like me to bring you one back?"

They both declined, and walked into the annex towards District Attorney Hughes office; not saying a word to each other as they walked down the hall. DA Hughes grabbed his key and unlocked his office door, walked over to his desk, sat down and said, "Detective McKnight, what is it that you want to talk about?"

"Frank, it's just me and you. No need to put on airs for anyone; there are no cameras in the room. I know that you don't care about what happens to any of the people involved in this case."

Frank slammed his hand on the desk and said, "Wait, one minute! Who do you think you are talking to?"

Detective McKnight replied, "Like I said, we are the only two in the room. You have made it very clear, when you first came into office, that you have your eyes set on the Governor's chair. I need you to understand, that I will not allow you to use this case to further your agenda. This case is bigger than just Private Investigator Grey's murder. There was a young girl who was raped and murdered, and her family has been fighting for justice for over a decade. Frank...we have to do right by them and bring Bryan Simmons to justice."

District Attorney Hughes said, "Sean, have a seat. You had your piece, now let me have mine. Do you know why I became an attorney?"

"No."

District Attorney Hughes leaned against his desk and said, "because I was a victim of a horrible crime when I was a teenager. I was walking home from my job late one evening; it was the first job I ever had—bagging groceries at a corner store—when a group of thugs robbed me. I didn't put up a fight, but that didn't stop them from beating me up. When it was over, I had to get 25 stitches in my head, and they broke my nose. Do you know the first thing that the cops asked me?

They asked why was *I* in that neighborhood, and if I was there to buy drugs or in a gang? I felt firsthand how it was to be treated different. I didn't understand why my family and I had to prove that I did nothing wrong and was not involved in any illegal activity, that may have put me in the wrong place, at the wrong time. When I asked my father why I was being treated like a criminal and not a victim, he told me, "Son, black folks just don't receive the same treatment sometimes when it comes to the law." I didn't accept that then, and I don't except that now. So, you are right; I am ambitious, and every case that I decide to prosecute, is purposeful and planned. I will be in that Governor's chair, because I plan to make changes that we can't make from the positions we are in today. I want to make sure that what happened to me does not continue to happen to other people."

Detective McKnight began to feel guilty for the assumptions that he had made regarding the district attorney. They had known each other for years, but he had never heard the DA's story before.

District Attorney Hughes walked over to Detective McKnight, standing face-to-face and said, "You don't have to like me or respect me, but don't ever say that I don't care about a victim."

Detective McKnight turned to walk away, then paused and said, "I hear you, and I am sorry that you had to experience that. Now, I need you to prove that you are more than just talk. Do the right thing, man!"

Walking out of the annex, Detective McKnight called Sheriff Walker to tell him he would be at the police station. Sheriff Walker said that he would join Detective McKnight in a bit; he was enjoying walking around sightseeing.

# CHAPTER 33

Detective McKnight barely sat down in his chair, when there was a knock at his office door. He got up and opened it; there was a short, stout lady there with a manila envelope in her hand. She said, "Detective Sean McKnight?"

He replied, "Yes."

She said, "You have been served."

He opened the envelope and couldn't believe it. Shelia was really going through with this—it was really over; these were papers for divorce. He slowly walked back to his desk, while trying to wrap his mind around how they got to that point. He had loved Shelia for as long as he could remember. After everything that was going on, he still loved her.

There was another knock on the door. McKnight shoved the papers into his desk drawer and said, "Come in."

Sheriff Walker came in, and so did the smell of onions and sauerkraut.

Detective McKnight said, "I smell that you enjoyed your hotdogs."

He replied, "Yes sir! So much so, that I grabbed two more on my way to your office."

Detective McKnight's coffee cup began to shake from the vibration of his phone that was sitting on his desk. He looked at it; there was a text message from District Attorney Hughes: *Meeting with Bryan Simmons and his attorney is set for 4:00 p.m. I'll meet you there.*

---

Detective McKnight and Sheriff Walker pulled up to the jail and sat in the car. The engine began to idle, and the windows frosted over.

Sheriff Walker said, "I can't wait to get back home to good ole Tennessee. I don't know how you folks deal with this cold."

Detective McKnight laughed and said "I don't how we do it either."

Pulling in quickly in the spot next to them, was a shiny blue Tesla. District Attorney Hughes stepped out in a light brown, wool Burberry coat.

As they walked down the halls of the jail to the conference room, Detective McKnight's heart started racing, thinking about Bryan Simmons and all the families he had destroyed. Some people are in jail because they were in the wrong place at the wrong time. Others made one bad mistake and must pay for it for the rest of their lives; and still others are there because of some miscarriage of justice. Then, you have the people like Bryan Simmons. Hard core criminals— the scum of the earth. He is a predator, and his only purpose in life is to hunt and hurt others.

Detective McKnight couldn't wait to see the expression on Bryan Simmons' face when he hears about the evidence that they have, and how they connected him to the unsolved murder in Tennessee. That arrogant smirk on his face, turning into a look of fear, when he finds out that they were going to try to extradite him to Tennessee, so he could face the death penalty.

They entered the conference room, and there sat Andre Williams a.k.a Bryan Simmons, along with his sleazy, beady-eyed attorney.

Andre sneered, "Hello, gentlemen; long time, no see. Are you here to make that deal? I'm ready to tell you everything you need to know about my love, Morgan."

District Attorney Hughes said, "Ok, Andre...but first, we have a few formalities that we need to discuss."

Andre looked at his attorney and said, "What formalities?" His attorney shrugged his shoulders.

District Attorney Hughes said, "Well, first we need to put your name on the record...so, can you please tell us what that is?"

Andre looked at his attorney, who tells him to go ahead and answer. Andre said, "My name is Andre Williams."

District Attorney Hughes replied, "Do you have any aliases that you would like to put on the record? Have you ever been known by any other name?"

Andre said, "No."

District Attorney Hughes put his pen down and said, "We will no longer be making any deal with you, sir. If you can't be honest about your name, I can't trust anything that comes out of your mouth."

Andre's attorney bemoaned, "What are you talking about? He gave you his legal name!"

District Attorney Hughes replied, "I also asked if he ever went by any other names, and he said, 'No,' and we know that is a lie... isn't that correct, Mr. Bryan Simmons?"

Andre's smirk turned into a smile. He sat up straight, as if another person was taking over his body and said, "You think you know me? You know nothing! You sit up here in your expensive suit and fancy job, and want to look down on me."

Andre's attorney said, "What is going on here?"

"New evidence has come to light," replied District Attorney Hughes, "and we will be charging Andre Williams a.k.a Bryan Simmons with murder here; and then he will be extradited to Tennessee, to face capital murder charges for the rape and murder of a 16-year-old girl."

Andre stood up and lunged at the District Attorney. Sheriff Walker got up and tackled him to the ground.

He yelled, "McKnight, I can use some help here! He is as strong as an Ox!"

McKnight ran over and helped Walker subdue Andre.

Detective McKnight, looking down at Andre eye to eye said, "Where is that smirk now? I can't wait to come to Tennessee and watch them put you down, like the filthy dog that you are."

The guards started to run into the room; they pulled Andre up to his feet and slammed him against the wall. When he calmed down, the guards sat him back into the chair and stood behind him.

Andre said, "I'm ready to give you a full confession. I will tell you everything; just don't let them take me back to Tennessee."

Andre's attorney said, "Andre, I would advise you not to say another word, until we have an agreement in writing."

Andre said, "Shut up. You can leave; I no longer need your services."

His attorney stood up and said, "Andre, again, I advise against this; but if this is what you want, I'll leave."

Shaking his head, Andre's attorney left the room.

Andre said, "Where would you like me to start? Do you want me to tell you how I lured Kasey out of the arcade that night? Do you want to know how I found Robin, and how she led me to Morgan? Or should I tell you about the last conversation that I had with that nosey private investigator?"

District Attorney Hughes opened his briefcase and pulled out a pocket-sized tape recorder; then he said, "For the record, let's start with your name."

He replied, "My name is Bryan Simmons a.k.a Andre Williams."

District Attorney Hughes said, "Mr. Simmons, do you waive your right of counsel?"

He replied, "Yes."

District Attorney Hughes continued, "Have you been coerced in any way into the confession that you are about to give?"

He replied, "No."

"Ok, go ahead and tell us about the murder of Private Investigator Grey, and the rape and murder of the young girl in Tennessee."

Detective McKnight interrupted, "Kasey...her name was Kasey, and she was a sweet and kind girl who loved her family. She was a straight A student, who played varsity basketball and had the dream to be a teacher when she grew up...and you stole that from her."

Bryan sat up, slammed his shackled hands on the table, licked his lips, and began to tell the story. He said that he and Jeremy Knotts had both been watching Kasey every summer she would come and stay with her family. Jeremy finally decided that he would try to talk to Kasey the night he saw her at the arcade. Kasey liked Jeremy too, so she went outside willingly with him. They started kissing, and Bryan said he walked up to her and said that he wanted a kiss too. Kasey said, "No," and said she was going to tell her aunt and her cousins that he tried to kiss her...then she started to walk back into the arcade.

Bryan said that he grabbed her arm—because nobody tells him no— and he and Jeremy dragged her to the alley and raped her. Bryan told her that if she told anyone, he would kill her and her family. He reminded her that it would be easy to do, since he was friends with her cousin and spent the night often. Kasey told him that she didn't care, and that she was telling. She got up and tried to run away, and Bryan grabbed and choked her, and then started to beat her until she stopped moving. He told Jeremy to grab her feet, and they threw her in the dumpster. Bryan said he lit a cigarette, and both he and Jeremy began to smoke, as they walked away.

Private Investigator Grey never gave up investigating the hit and run of Jeremy Knotts; he stayed in touch with Bryan, because he was a close friend of the family. After Jeremy's mom died, he had no one else to keep updated on the case. Private Investigator Grey told Bryan that he was sure that the three girls from Ohio were guilty, but he couldn't get enough evidence. Bryan was in Private Investigator Grey's office, when he found the contact information for Robin Harris and Morgan Waters.

Bryan said that Grey had discovered a box of Jeremy's that was among some things that his mother had given PI Grey before she died. Unbeknownst to Grey, there was a letter in the box that Jeremy had written to his mother. In the letter, Jeremy confessed to the brutal rape and murder of Kasey. In the letter, he said that he felt really bad. He really liked Kasey, but he went along with his friend, and there was no turning back. Jeremy didn't say who the friend was.

One evening, Grey was going through all of Jeremy's things for the last time and decided that he would not be able to solve the murder and put the girls at the scene of the crime. He had a friend at the FBI, who solved cold cases; so, he was going to send everything to him to see if they could solve this. He began going through the box, and that's when he discovered the letter.

Bryan said that he packed up his car and headed towards Ohio...his only desire from that point forward, was to hunt down the three girls who were responsible for the death of his friend and to kill them. Jeremy and Bryan had been friends ever since Bryan had moved in with a foster family, in the town of Kinsee. Some of the town's kids would tease Bryan, and even though Jeremy was a few years younger, he would always stand up for him.

Bryan called the numbers that he had found in PI Grey's notes, and the only one who answered was Robin Harris. Bryan acted like he was a bill collector and told her that they had been sending her letters demanding payment, but she had not responded; and if she didn't send the payment, that they would take legal actions. He then told her the address they had on file; and she corrected him, giving her correct address. He sat outside her house and watched her for weeks, getting her routine down.

One day, he bumped into her at her the park, where she went every Saturday morning. He smiled—no one could resist his smile. He started a conversation with her, and from that day, on they were talking every day. He found out that she was in and out of drug rehab, and he became her confidant. One day, when she was feeling really bad and wanted to get high, he stayed with her the whole night, holding her and talking to her, until her urge had passed.

Bryan said he asked her why she was doing this to herself, and she told him it was because she was a horrible person, and the drugs were the only things that helped her forget. He reassured her that the load she was carrying was too heavy to carry on her own, and he would help her in any way that he could. Bryan confided in her that he had also done some horrible, even unforgivable things himself, so whatever she had done, she could tell him, and he would not judge her. Robin then told Bryan the story of what happened that summer in Tennessee.

Robin begin crying uncontrollably and told Bryan that she needed a fix. He wanted to strangle her right there, but he decided that she deserved a worse fate. So, he went out, bought heroine, came back to her apartment, and gave it to her. He then left, and returned two days later, and Robin was in the condition that he hoped she would be in. He told her to tell him everything about the other two girls. She told him how Shawna killed herself, and that Morgan was a big-shot attorney in Rhode Island. For the next three months, he stayed with Robin, learning all he could about Morgan; all the while making sure that Robin stayed high.

Bryan decided that Robin would eventually die from an overdose, or some other way that junkies died. He left, and headed towards Rhode Island to kill Morgan. He found her law firm and started stalking her for a few weeks. Once he had her routine down, he ran into her at her favorite coffee shop. His plan was to follow her home and strangle her, but there was something about her. She was so beautiful, and he couldn't help himself. He then decided that he had to have her; and that he would ruin her life, and then kill her.

The night of the engagement party, he saw Private Investigator Grey, who told Bryan that he was going to expose him to Morgan. Grey told him that he knew what he had done, and once he had enough evidence, he was going to spend the rest of his life in prison.

Bryan saw Grey heading out from the dinner, and soon after, Morgan left the room. Bryan followed him out of the back door, and they started arguing; then Bryan pulled out a knife and stabbed him over and over and over. Right then, Morgan walked up. She and Bryan argued, and she ran over to Grey. Bryan walked up behind her, she stood up and turned around to face him, and he started to choke her. He watched her eyes go towards the back of her head, and he kept squeezing until her body went limp. Then he threw her into the swimming pool, thinking she was dead.

Bryan said that he figured he would take care of them both. He ran when he heard someone coming towards the back yard.

---

The room was silent. Sheriff Walker got up and left to get some fresh air. District Attorney Hughes and Detective McKnight looked at one another in horror.

Detective McKnight said, "I have one question...are you sorry for any of this?"

Bryan looked at him with his cold, dark eyes and said, "My only regret, is that I didn't finish Morgan off." He smiled and sat back in his seat.

District Attorney Hughes cut off the recorder and said to Bryan, "I will keep my promise...you will not be sent to Tennessee."

Detective McKnight jumped up and said, "You have got to be kidding me, Frank! He has no remorse! Killing people is a game to him."

Frank said, "Detective, that is enough. Sit down, and let me finish."

District Attorney Hughes faced Bryan and said, "I have been a prosecutor for many years, and what I do know is that people like you are predators—monsters—and once a monster gets a taste for something, he has to have it again and again. Most monsters don't stop until they are caught and put down. Your DNA is with the FBI, and they are going to search their database for unsolved rapes and murders; and if and when they connect you to another crime, we are going to make sure we find a way to stick a needle in your arm...you can believe that."

District Attorney Hughes and Detective McKnight left the room.

Detective McKnight reached out his hand and said, "Frank, I never saw that coming. You scared me for a moment there...I have a new respect for you."

He replied, "I told you that I became a prosecutor to help those who can't help themselves, and those who are ignored by the system; and I think that was accomplished today." District Attorney Hughes put on his fedora, that matched his Burberry trench coat, and walked out the door.

Detective McKnight drove to the Calloway's house to tell Morgan that she was free to go home, and that she was no longer a suspect...and that Bryan confessed to everything. He also told her that she would have to go to Tennessee to face any charges that might be brought against her there. He said that Sheriff Walker was going to talk to the DA and let her know that Morgan played an important role in helping uncover the unsolved rape and murder in their town.

Mr. Calloway assured Morgan that he and Jean would support her, no matter what. Mr. Calloway said, "So, son, now that this case is over, what's next for you?"

Detective McKnight replied, "I decided that I want to help the voiceless and those families who are waiting for justice. I put in my two weeks' notice at the police station. I talked to a buddy of Private Investigator Grey's at the FBI, who oversees a division that helps local police departments solve unsolved murders. He told me he has a spot available, and I'm going to take it. Right now, I have a plane to catch. I'm going back to Tennessee to tell Ms. Kingston that we finally caught her niece's rapist and murderer; and let Mrs. Grey know how her husband helped to solve two unsolved murders, and that he died a hero."

Detective McKnight walked over to Morgan, held her hand and said, "Your past can only define you if you let it. Every day that you live, you can be better and do better. You can make a difference in other people's lives. You cannot continue to hold onto the past; you need to forgive yourself and live the rest of your life with the sole purpose of being the best version of yourself that you can be. I believe in you."

A tear dropped down Morgan's cheek, as she watched Detective McKnight walk out of the door. She turned around, wiped the tear off her face, and smiled. Morgan went to her room and began to stare at herself in the mirror. Then, she went into her purse and pulled out her red lipstick; she put it on and kissed the mirror and began to laugh uncontrollably. She went into her briefcase, pulled out her one-way ticket to the Maldives and set it on the bed, alongside her passport.

She grabbed a piece of paper and sat at the desk, and began to write a letter to Mr. Calloway:

*Dear Mr. Calloway,*

*I am writing this letter, because I have to get a few things off of my chest. First of all, I want to thank you for representing me and believing in me but your services are no longer needed. See, ever since I was a little girl, I knew how to bat my eyes and smile, and make people believe me...I could get away with anything.*

*Obviously, I see I still have it. I am a black swan, but not the one you pictured me as. I turned tragedy into fuel. Fuel to destroy everyone and anything that could stop me from having what I wanted. I decided that I would never be anyone's victim ever again, and no one would ever take what rightly belongs to me.*

*My father was a drunk, who didn't protect me from his brother, who molested me for years; and my mother left me. That meant the only person I have, and I have always had, was me.*

*The night Shawna died, I came home from class, and she was sitting on the bed crying. She was online looking at a newspaper article from Tennessee. The article was about a private investigator who had started looking into the murder of a hit and run victim. In the article, the mother pleaded for whomever was responsible, to come forward. Shawna said she had called the private investigator and left a message for him to call her back. I found a letter on her bed that she had written to her parents, confessing to the hit in run. She told her parents that she wanted to tell the police, but Robin and I talked her out of it.*

*I asked her if she wanted something to drink to calm down, because she was so upset, and she said, "Yes." I dropped two of my sleeping pills in the alcohol and waited until she fell asleep. Then, I filled the bathtub and helped her into it; she was too out of it to fight. I drowned her, and then took the razor and slit her wrist. I told her that I would not let her ruin my life.*

*I changed my clothes, put the wet, bloody clothes in a bag, and threw them in a dumpster, as I was on my way to my study group. I went to the group, had pizza, went back home, and pretended to find her. She was such a weak and pathetic person; the only thing she needed to do was keep her mouth shut, and she couldn't even do that.*

*I did recognize Private Investigator Grey. He came to Ohio and interviewed Robin and I our freshman year. We both acted like we knew nothing, and there was no evidence, besides the phone call he* received from Shawna saying had some information; and I guess there was a waitress who remembered seeing three girls stop at her diner in a car with Ohio plates.

Private Investigator Grey called me at the firm the night before my engagement party, and said he was in town and wanted to talk to me about some new evidence regarding the hit and run. After that conversation, I knew he had to die. I couldn't take the chance of him exposing my involvement in the hit and run. I told him that I couldn't talk and invited him to our engagement party.

I was talking to Andre, when Grey walked in. I excused myself from Andre and walked over and started to talk to him. Andre looked surprised when the PI walked in. I made sure that I looked at Andre several times while we were talking. Grey told me that he knew that I was somehow involved in the hit and run, but he was not there about that. He said he was looking into the unsolved murder of some girl in 2004. I told him that I could not talk and asked him to meet me outside by the guest room so we could talk privately. I walked away from him, looking upset, and that's when Andre went over there to him, and they had a few words.

When I was talking to Andre, I told him that the man said he was private investigator, asking me if I knew anyone named Bryan Simmons. I could see Andre's mind working overtime. I told him that I told the man I did not.

During dinner, I wrote on a piece of paper, "Meet me outside by the guest house." I waited until I saw Andre walking back into the room, and I stuck the paper under my plate, then excused myself when Andre sat down. I knew he would look to see what I was trying to hide.

At the guest house, Andre and the PI started arguing, and then Andre pulled out a knife and began to stab Grey. Andre turned and looked at me, and told me he had been waiting to do this, then he started to strangle me. The next thing I knew I was being pulled out of the water.

I knew that Andre would try to kill Grey to keep him quiet. I *didn't think he would try to kill me. I guess that is the price that you have to pay sometimes. When I was in the hospital, I felt relieved because Grey was dead, and my secret was still safe. That was, until I heard about Robin going to the police.*

*I flew down to visit her the weekend that I told you and Jean that I needed to be by myself. When I saw Robin, she was a pitiful shell of herself. I told her to keep her mouth shut, and that I would send her money to feed her drug habit, since her aunt and everyone else had cut her off. Robin told me about the time she had spent with Andre, and how she told him everything about the hit and run...and that he had her go to Detective McKnight. I made sure she stayed high and not credible. Eventually, she ended back up in rehab. It was perfect, because she was not available to talk to Detective McKnight.*

*Since the police had someone sitting on my house, I used that opportunity to call Andre and told him I knew who he was; and I was going to expose him. I knew that would lure him back to try to kill me. My plan was to shoot him and kill him first, but he knocked the gun out of my hand and started to choke me. I was relieved when I saw Detective McKnight burst into my room and pushed the gun under my bed with my foot.*

*My hope was that Andre would struggle with Detective McKnight and be shot, but that didn't happen. When I was arrested, and you suggested that I take the polygraph, I knew I would pass; because even though I put the murder in motion, I never told Andre to kill him.*

*I have one more thing that I need to do. I have to go back to Ohio and take care of the person who turned me into who I am; and that's my uncle, the one who took away my innocence.*

*They say confession is good for the soul, so thank you for allowing me to get all these things off my chest. Maybe now I can sleep and not be awaken by those blue eyes that have haunted my sleep. By the time you receive this letter I will be gone and you will never see me again.*

*XOXO*

*Morgan*

Morgan put the letter in her purse and walked downstairs. She said her goodbyes to Mr. and Mrs. Calloway, and thanked them for letting her stay with them.

Mr. Calloway said, "You are welcome, Morgan. I will see you Monday."

With a smile Morgan said, "I will see you Monday."

She walked out the door, got into the Uber and said, "Take me to Green International Airport."

# Acknowledgments

I would like to express my sincere love and appreciation to my husband Patrick and my children Kierra, Kevin, and Kendall, and mother Brenda.

I also want to thank my siblings, nieces, and nephews for their unwavering love and support. A special thanks to my friends who supported and encouraged me through this process.

I want to give a big thanks to my editors Rachel and Tameka I could not have done this without you.

# About the Author

Dee McQueen was born in 1975 in Ypsilanti, Michigan. Her love of writing began as a way to express her feelings. Deanna's love of mysteries started when she was a child and would watch Columbo with her father. She is the mother of 3 beautiful children and 1 grandson. She also has a business, By Deezign Mysteries, writing and hosting murder mystery parties.